George John Whyte-Melville

Contraband

Vol. 2

George John Whyte-Melville

Contraband
Vol. 2

ISBN/EAN: 9783337379858

Printed in Europe, USA, Canada, Australia, Japan

Cover: Foto ©Andreas Hilbeck / pixelio.de

More available books at **www.hansebooks.com**

CONTRABAND;

OR,

A Losing Hazard.

By G. J. WHYTE-MELVILLE,

AUTHOR OF "DIGBY GRAND," "CERISE," "THE WHITE ROSE," &c.

IN TWO VOLUMES.

VOL. II.

LONDON:
CHAPMAN AND HALL, 193, PICCADILLY.
1871.

CONTENTS OF VOL. II.

CONTRABAND;

OR, A LOSING HAZARD.

CHAPTER XVII.

DISTRACTIONS.

Mrs. Lascelles, like many of her sex, entertained a high opinion of her own medical skill in all ailments of mind or body. If your finger ached she would produce an absurd little box, the size of a Geneva watch, from which, with an infinitesimal gold spoon, like a bodkin, she proceeded to give you a strong dose, consisting of two white atoms not so large as pins' heads, dissolved in a glass of pure water, which they neither flavoured nor coloured, nor otherwise affected in the least. Repeating this elfin discipline two or three times with the utmost gravity, she would have been exceedingly mortified, and almost offended, if you had not declared yourself better forthwith. And it is but fair to say that I never heard of any one being worse for the prescriptions she dispensed with such confidence and liberality.

But if the pain was in your heart this general practitioner buckled on her armour with yet greater alacrity, and confronted the enemy on a far more vigorous system of tactics. She refrained indeed, wisely enough, from prematurely assaulting his stronghold, but attacked his outworks one by one with unflinching determination, so that the citadel, deprived on all sides of its supports, wavered, collapsed, and surrendered at discretion.

One of the most powerful engines with which she battered, so to speak, the obstinate fortresses garrisoned by such tried veterans as Memory, Pique, and Disappointment, was a "little gaiety," by which Mrs. Lascelles understood a round of London amusements and continual change of scene. "Sympathy, my dear," she would say, with a comical little sigh and shake of her dainty head, "sympathy from those who have felt sorrow, and going about—to good places, of course—with dancing, you know, and plenty of partners, will cure anything. *Anything!* I assure you, for I've tried it; except, perhaps, a broken neck!"

In pursuance, then, of this extremely plausible theory, it was not long after the events described in the last chapter, that Miss Hallaton found herself sitting next Mrs. Lascelles in a box at the Opera, hoping, no doubt, for that distraction from sorrow which I fear is seldom found in music, mirth, or gaiety; but which is rarely sought in vain by the pillow of suffering, in the house of mourning, under any roof or in any situation where we can lend a willing hand at the great cable of brotherly love and unselfish effort, which alone hauls the ship's company into port at last.

It seems to me that sights and sounds of beauty serve but to add a cruel poison to the sting; whereas honest, unremitting toil, provides us a certain opiate; and active charity towards others draws gradually the venom from our wound.

Helen had suffered acutely. The girl's pride was humbled to the dust, and even that infliction was not the worst. Her gods had deceived her, and her idols proved to be but clay. Frank Vanguard's conduct was more than fickle, more than heartless; it seemed actually brutal and unmanly! Since her reply to the letter in which he asked her to become his wife, he had never been near her, had held no communication with her family nor herself, but had avoided them all with a persistence insulting as it was unaccountable.

Whatever reasons he might have, she felt his conduct was utterly inexcusable, and Helen endured that bitterest of all punishments, the conviction not only that her love was without return, but that she had bestowed it on an unworthy object; had misconceived the very nature, mistaken the very identity of him whom she once felt proud to know so thoroughly, whom she imagined no one thus knew but herself.

"I thought him so different!" In that simple sentence—said by how many, and how bitterly!—lurked all the sorrow, all the humiliation, all the despair. The man she loved had never really existed. She must teach herself to forget this dream, this delusion, as if it had never been. With woman's fortitude of endurance, woman's decency of courage, Helen fought her battle, hid her wounds, and swallowed her tears, but the struggle told on her severely. Sir Henry, cursing late hours and hot rooms, talked of taking his daughter back to the country. Even Jin's heart smote her when she marked the pale face, the drooping gestures, the sad, weary looks; while Mrs. Lascelles, insisting on her own treatment of a malady she was persuaded she alone could cure, took every opportunity of administering amusement in large doses, and esteemed no part of her regimen more efficacious than these long hours of heat, glare, noise, imprisonment, and musical stupefaction, spent at the Italian Opera.

So Helen, watching the business of the stage

with eyes from which the tears would *not* keep back, while those thrilling strains rose and fell in the outcry of remorseful passion, or the wail of hopeless, yet undying love, wondered vaguely why there should be all this sorrow upon earth, springing, apparently, from the purest and most elevated instincts of the human heart. She forgot that a time would come hereafter, perhaps on this side the grave, when the misery that was eating into her own young life must seem no less unreasonable, no less unreal, than that of the harmonious lady yonder, in pearls and white satin, who would take her place at supper in an hour, with spirits and appetite unimpaired by the breaking heart that, flying mellifluously to her lips in this intricate *cavatina*, brought down on her a rainbow shower of bouquets, followed by a thunderstorm of applause. "That *is* singing!" said Miss Ross, from the back of the box, drawing a long breath of intense enjoyment, the enjoyment of the artist who appreciates as well as admires. "Rose, why didn't I bring a bouquet? I'd throw my head at her if it would take off!"

Mrs. Lascelles laughed, and made a sign signifying "Hush!" while Miss Ross whispered over Helen's shoulder—"Isn't it *too* delightful, dear? In my opinion music's the only thing worth living for!"

Helen, who esteemed nothing much worth living for at that moment, responded with modified enthusiasm, and turned languidly to the stage. Just then the box-door opened; and she knew, though he was behind her, and had not spoken a syllable, that it admitted Frank Vanguard!

He couldn't keep away! Of course he would not have allowed that any part of this crowded house held for him the slightest attraction.

Fidgeting in the stalls, and getting Helen's well-remembered profile within range of his opera-glasses, it was only natural he should tell himself she could never be more to him than a humiliating memory, a cause of gratitude for his narrow escape. It was also natural that he should take his good manners severely to task for negligence, in not having called lately on

Mrs. Lascelles, and should scout the notion of being kept out of her box by anybody in the world, man or woman! So, looking paler than usual, and, for once in his life, almost pompous in his embarrassment, he tapped at the door, and found himself stumbling over a delicate little satin-shod foot, belonging to Miss Ross, of whose presence, to do him justice, till he made this ungainly entrance, he had not the slightest suspicion.

"It's a good omen!" thought that quaint and speculative young person, while *her* heart too was beating faster than common. "I shall trip you up at last, sir; and what a fall I'll give you!" But she reflected also that they would probably go down together; and there was something not unpleasant in the apprehension.

Frank recovered himself sufficiently to greet Mrs. Lascelles with customary politeness, and made Helen a ceremonious bow, without offering to shake hands. She construed the omission into a studied and gratuitous slight.

So the poor girl turned once more to the stage, leaning her cheek on her hand, and wondering sadly, almost humbly, what she had done to be so punished, tried to interest herself in the progress of the opera.

A tenor, swelling in black velvet, was expressing intense adoration of some object unknown, possibly the great chandelier, at which he trilled and quavered with unflagging persistency—lifting to it eyes, eyebrows, chest, and shoulders, rising on his toes, as if, like the skylark soaring and singing towards the light, he would fain project himself, his voice, his trunk-breeches, and his dearest affections, right through the roof!

Nor did he seem in the slightest degree influenced by suspicion or dismay, though the stage, becoming gradually darkened, filled rapidly with assassins, all wearing black cloaks, black masks, black gloves, brandishing poniards, and bursting forth—as was extremely natural in a band of paid murderers stealing on their victim—into a magnificent and deafening chorus, such as caused the very curls of the Conductor to vibrate on his head, while he waved his baton to and fro in spasmodic frenzy, the crisis of a musical delirium.

It was Jin's opportunity. From her dark corner those black eyes flashed like lamps, while she murmured, under cover of the ophicleide and the big drum—

"You've never been to see us, Captain Vanguard. Rose has missed you sadly, and—and—so have I."

A vacant chair stood by her own, so close, that her gown partly covered its cushion. There was obvious invitation in her gesture, while she removed the intrusive fold, and Frank dropped willingly enough into that vacant seat.

Wounded, sore, reckless, angry with one woman, he was in a mood to render the attractions of such another as Miss Ross extremely dangerous. His attention being taken off his own grievances, the cessation of pain was in itself delightful; and I fear he had too little generosity to forbear the petty triumph of showing Miss Hallaton that others could care for him even if she did not. Besides, the act of flirting with such a professor as Jin in the dark corner of an opera-box, however dangerous, was, in itself, no unpleasant pastime; so, while Helen, cold and sick at heart, suffered herself to be deafened by chorus and orchestra, Frank, to use his own expression, "went in a perisher, and made tremendous running with Miss Ross!"

She was an experienced angler, so perfect in the art that being in earnest rather increased her skill than otherwise. The popularity of our Italian Opera is not entirely due to its music, the best and the highest paid for in Europe. Its boxes form also a convenient territory for the prosecution of those skirmishes, which would become actual warfare but for the nature of the ground on which they take place. There are fair and dazzling visions, there are soft, sad sounds—most intoxicating when softest and saddest. There is bright glare on others, semi-obscurity for ourselves. There are sympathy, juxta-position, a common object of interest, a necessity for whispers, and a propriety in absolute silence, which is in itself the strongest possible stimulant to conversation. Above all, there is a certain sentiment of isolation, the result of being shut up together for a definite period, that renders people mutually attractive; just as no man alive can accompany a woman, however ugly, for a long sea voyage, and not fall in love with her to a certainty.

"You don't, and you *know* you don't!" whispered Jin, in answer to some wild remark of Frank's, drowned for all ears but her own in an outrageous crash of brass instruments. "Though, mind, I won't have you fancy for a moment that I lump you in with the others, tie you all up in a bunch, and label you 'poison.' No, I shall not give you my poor gardenia. You'll take it on to Lady Clearwell's, I dare say. But it will never get any farther than the first pretty woman you dance with. Water! Pooh! It would wither, poor thing, and much you'd care for it, then! Well, if you *really* promise—— No. I won't. I never did in my life, and I won't begin! You needn't move, it's only Goldie. Now *that's* a faithful admirer, if you like!"

It was indeed none other but this devoted swain, who, meekly entering, and paying homage stiffly enough to Mrs. Lascelles, seated himself between that lady and Helen, but afforded the former far the largest share of his attention and indisputable remarks on things in general.

The mistress of the box could not be said to be disappointed, though she wished it was somebody else, for her glasses were even now fixed on that somebody's drooping aristocratic old head, a dozen feet below her. Why did he not come up? She owed him the less grudge for this neglect, that she had a strong conviction Sir Henry Hallaton was fast asleep in his stall.

Mrs. Lascelles stifled a sigh.

"It's up-hill work—very!" she said to her own heart. "And I'm making this other poor fellow sadly wretched. He's like the people one reads about in a novel. He never complains. I wish he would! I wish he'd scold me well, and tell me what a beast I am!"

Touching his arm with her fan, while she made some trifling observation, it cut her to the quick to observe how his face brightened up, like a dog's at the voice of its master; and for the first time Mrs. Lascelles found herself entertaining a vague suspicion that it might be unwise as well as unfeeling to throw away so much confiding adoration, to barter a reality that would last her lifetime, for a mere fancy, less tangible and less permanent than a dream. So, with half-a-dozen kind words, meaning nothing, she lifted this simple young man to the seventh heaven of transport, reaping, from her own act, the quiet satisfaction that follows such deeds of benevolence and common humanity.

Meanwhile, Frank had risen to go. Carefully abstaining from the slightest glance in Miss Hallaton's direction, he took an exceedingly affectionate leave of Miss Ross, and resumed his stall, which was next to that of Sir Henry, fastening a gardenia, with some little pretension, in his button-hole.

"Been on the war-path," thought Sir Henry,

waking up from a doze and observing this lately-won decoration. "Quick work. Taken a scalp already, and hanging it on his belt." Then he remembered his own daughter was in the house, and meditated grimly on the deadly penalties he would exact from any man who should be so rash as to trifle with Helen; consoled, however, by the reflection that she was the last girl in the world to yield even so light a trophy as a flower to one who had not earned it in honourable and legitimate warfare.

"What's the attraction, Jin?" asked Mrs. Lascelles, with something of irritation in her tone. "You've never taken your glasses off one spot in the stalls for the last ten minutes! Will you share the object amongst us, or must you keep it all to yourself?"

Miss Ross was never at a loss.

"It's the tower of Babel, dear," she answered, good humouredly, "before the confusion of tongues. Did you ever see such a head! There, two rows behind Sir Henry Hallaton. The woman in pink, with all those beads wound round her, bangles on her arms, and, I do believe, a fish-bone through her nose! I can see it, I'm sure, when she turns this way!" Thus Jin, with her glasses in her lap, with mirth and mischief in her eyes, to all appearance with no sentiment but ridicule in her heart.

Miss Ross deserved credit, I think, for unscrupulous invention and readiness of resource, also for the quickness with which she pounced on the woman in pink, a respectable matron, whose head-gear, modelled after that of a notorious Parisian impropriety, was simply such as she saw worn by ladies of her own station and repute every night of her life.

Jin would have studied this apparition perhaps more attentively, but that her whole soul was projecting itself, as it were, through her glasses, towards Frank Vanguard and his gardenia. She did not regret giving it him now. She was falling horribly in love with him. How she would have hated Helen, she thought, but that she could afford to pity her!

I have said this enthusiast *really* enjoyed an

opera, loving *fine* even more dearly than *pretty* music.

Deferring, therefore, till to-morrow the laying of plans, calculation of chances, that laborious train of reflection in which she knew too well she must collect the resources of her head to attain the desire of her heart, she sat back in her chair, and abandoned herself to one of those dreams which are perhaps the most ecstatic of all visions vouchsafed to us poor children of clay.

To repose unobserved in a corner, to drink in sounds of more than mortal sweetness, on which the soul, linked to one dear image, like Paolo in the arms of Francesca, floats away, away through the realms of space, into the fabulous regions of unchanging, unadulterated love,—is not this a happiness to which the joy of fruition, the content of security, must seem sadly tame and insipid, to which the "sober certainty of waking bliss" is but vulgar reality, clogging the wings of impossible romance?

And now the performance drew to a close. The tenor had sung his *aria* of triumphant villany, and his *solo* of despairing remorse. The *basso*, having cursed through the whole gamut in exceedingly correct time, had fallen on his knees at the footlights, tearing a white wig, after the approved pattern of King Lear. Priests, soldiers, friars, courtiers, townsmen, stately nobles, and smiling peasant-girls, thronged the entire depth of the stage, while above the motley crowd waved and flaunted symbols of religion, spoils of warfare, and the banner of France. The *prima donna*, venting shriek on shriek, with surprising shrillness and rapidity, had died in convulsions of unusual energy, and even repeated her demise, after an enthusiastic *encore;* the orchestra, becoming louder, fiercer, faster, with each successive bar, had worked up to the grand deafening and discordant crash, which is esteemed a worthy *finale* to all great compositions, and the curtain hovering to a fall, glasses were cased, white shoulders cloaked, both on and off the stage all acting was over, and the audience rose to go away.

Let us follow Mrs. Lascelles and her party, escorted only by the constant Goldthred, as they leave their box to attain the stairs, the crush-room, the carriage, and eventually the street.

We shall not need to hurry—their progress, gaining about a yard a minute, is slow and deliberate as a funeral. At the lowest step of the whole flight, Helen is aware of Frank Vanguard making his way through the crush, apparently with the intention of joining their party. In her distress, looking wildly round for help, she catches sight of her father's grizzled head above the surface; and, meeting his eye, telegraphs for assistance. Sir Henry, whose redeeming point is the care he takes of his daughter, makes no cessation of edging, sliding, bowing, and begging pardon, till he reaches her side, and thus places himself in a false position as regards the ladies he has lately left. They cling to him with annoying persistence, and he condemns himself, very forcibly too, though below his breath, more than once for having a daughter "out," and yet choosing to know such women as Mrs. Battersea and her sister, Kate Cremorne. He must not introduce them to Mrs. Lascelles, as they obviously wish; he *will* not introduce them to Helen, though they would like this too; and how can he ignore them completely, when he is engaged to supper this very night at their house? With all his careless selfishness, it annoyed Sir Henry exceedingly to be guilty of a rudeness or unkindness towards anyone, and he formed more good resolutions to avoid doubtful society for the future in the half-dozen paces he waded through that stream of muslin four feet deep, and all the colours of the rainbow, than he had made, and broken, in his whole life before.

Ere he could accost Helen, however, assistance arrived from an unexpected quarter. Picard, who was just as sure to be at the Opera as any one of the fiddles in the orchestra, recognised his fellow-travellers from Windsor with a profound and enthusiastic bow, followed by a smiling approach, in which his teeth, his whiskers, his grin, and his stealthy yet confident demeanour, proclaimed the "tiger" of social life, not wanting in some of the attributes belonging to his nobler namesake, the terror of the jungle.

In another stride he would have offered his arm to Helen, but Mrs. Lascelles, warned by Sir Henry's eye, interposed, and seeing no other way of saving her charge, with a devotion almost maternal, cast off from Goldthred and seized it herself.

"Take care of Helen!" she whispered in the latter's ear, while the flowers in her wreath brushed his very cheek. "This man mustn't take her—you understand! Come to-morrow to luncheon."

The whisper and its purport made him quite happy; Mrs. Lascelles had also the satisfaction of observing something like displeasure cloud Sir Henry's eyes as they rested on herself and her *impromptu* cavalier.

"If he's cross it shows he *cares*," was her first thought. "Ah! he'll never care like the *other one*,"—her second, and that which remained longest in her mind.

The "other one," in the meantime, walked meekly on towards the carriage with Helen tucked under his elbow, thus freeing Sir Henry from his embarrassment, and leaving him at leisure to devote his attentions to Mrs. Battersea, who was, indeed, by no means inclined to let him off.

Mrs. Lascelles followed on the arm of Picard, who behaved as well as he could, though he would rather have taken Helen; these were succeeded by Jin and Frank Vanguard, apparently very well pleased with each other and thoroughly disposed to accept the situation.

I know not what Frank whispered, but gather that it was something complimentary by his companion's answer.

"We're not the only ones!" said Jin, looking up from under a scarlet hood, like a bewitching gipsy.

"How do you mean?" asked Frank, innocently enough.

"Don't you see your old love and Mr. Goldthred?" was the reply. "Confess now—honour! You *did* care for her once!"

"A little, perhaps," he answered lightly, though his lip quivered, and she saw it.

"But you don't now?" she pursued, leaning towards him with a gesture of confiding tenderness impossible to resist.

"You *know* I don't," he answered, and pressed the arm that rested on his own, gently but firmly to his heart.

She broke into one of those rare smiles by which, on occasion, she knew how to rivet her work so securely.

"It's a case, I'm sure!" she exclaimed. "They'll be a very happy couple, and I can wish her joy *now* with all my heart!"

CHAPTER XVIII.

ATTRACTIONS.

THERE are various phases of hospitality on which people depend for increase of social reputation and entertainment of their friends. One lady sets great store by her dinners, the excellence of her cook, the lighting and decorations of her table, the tact with which she selects her guests. Another believes it impossible to equal her "breakfasts," why so called, I am at a loss to explain, since they take place after luncheon. A third thinks this last-named meal forms the perfection of friendly intercourse, while a fourth stands or falls by the agreeable circle she gathers round her at afternoon tea. Mrs. Battersea affected none of these. She piqued herself exclusively on her suppers; and to sup with

Mrs. Battersea after the Opera was to form one of a circle more remarkable for gaiety, good humour, and general recklessness, than for wisdom, propriety of demeanour, or reputed respectability.

They were very pleasant, nevertheless, these little gatherings. She understood so thoroughly how they should be constituted, the quantity of guests, the quality of wines drank, and the dishes set on the table. You had some difficulty in finding her house, no doubt, even if you went in a hack-cab, for it lurked in those remoter regions of London which are to Belgravia what Belgravia must once have been to Grosvenor Square. She was a "settler," she said, and liked the wild, free life of the borders. When the real respectables, dowager peeresses and those sort of people, moved down to her, she would "up stick" and clear out farther west! Meantime the little house looked very charming, even at half-past twelve P.M. The delicate foliage of an acacia quivered in the light at its door; your foot trod the street pavement indeed, but your nostrils breathed the fragrance of hawthorn and hay-fields, not so very far off. A flagged passage through ten feet of garden led you into a beautiful little hall with tesselated pavement, globe lamps, statuettes, flower-boxes, a fountain, and a cockatoo. On your senses stole the heavy, subtle odour of incense, the soft strains of a self-playing pianoforte, far off in some room up-stairs. You were sure to be expected; no pompous auxiliary from Gunter's extorted your name, but the smoothest and lightest-footed of butlers received your overcoat and motioned you in silence towards a room, from the open door of which floods of light streamed across the carpeted passage, whence you heard the popping of corks, the *cliquetis d'assiettes*, the pleasant voices of women, the soft ripple of talk and laughter within.

You had time for scarcely a glance at that group after Watteau, that Leda in alabaster, the ormolu on velvet, the porcelain under glass, for, brushing the deep, soft carpet, with step noiseless as your conductor's, you entered an octagon room, brilliantly lighted, containing a round table, on which flowers and fruit were grouped in tasteful profusion, the whole set off by a circular lamp dependent from the ceiling, and so shaded as to throw its glare on grapes, geraniums, roses, glass and gold, table ornaments and china, glittering plate, and bubbling wine.

At this table were already seated some half-dozen noisy, pleasant individuals, when Sir Henry arrived. His entrance was the signal for a fresh burst of laughter, and a triumphant clapping of hands.

"You've won on both events, Kate," exclaimed Mrs. Battersea, making room for the belated guest by her side. "It was even betting you wouldn't come, Sir Henry. Kate shot us all round, and laid three to two you would be here before the soup was cold!"

"They thought you had been made safe, Sir Henry," said the last-named lady, whose specialty it was to speak very demurely and very distinctly. "But I knew better. Now, don't talk till you've had something to eat."

He took her advice and glanced round the

table while he sipped a clear soup—brown, strong, and restorative as sherry.

There were only two people he didn't know, a man and a woman: the former, stout, florid, bearded, deep-voiced, with the unmistakable artist type, being indeed a sculptor of no mean celebrity; the latter, wrinkled, faded, a snuff-taker, with false teeth and hair. She seemed witty and agreeable, however, fruitful in anecdote, deadly in repartee, with something of foreign buoyancy in manner.

She filled her glass, and emptied it too, pretty often. Sir Henry set her down for an Englishwoman naturalised in Paris.

The rest consisted of Picard, to whom he had lately been introduced, young Kilgarron, Frank Vanguard, and Mrs. Battersea's sister, the enterprising Kate Cremorne.

What the former had been fifteen years ago, the latter lady was now: hazel eyes, high colour, dazzling teeth, auburn hair, bright in manner, dress, and appearance. The elder sister exhausted all appliances of the toilet, to put the clock back those fifteen years and look like the younger, but in vain; nevertheless, such was the difference of their ages, that she regarded Kate less with a sister's jealousy than a mother's indulgent affection.

"So you backed me in, Miss Kate?" said the baronet, touching her glass lightly with his own, ere he drank a mouthful of champagne. "Knew I was to be depended on, didn't you? Just like a great stupid cockchafer blundering to the light. You're the light, you know, and I'm the cockchafer."

"You must be pretty well singed by this time!" answered Kate, laughing. "No; the others thought you wouldn't be allowed to get away; but I was sure you would come directly if anybody told you *not!*"

Mrs. Battersea attacked him on the other side.

"Confess, Sir Henry, you haven't heard the last of this from a certain lady whose name begins with an L. You *know* you won't dare call at No. 40 for a week!"

"Why?" he asked simply, and emptied his glass.

"Why, indeed!" answered the other. "She looked as black as thunder, and absolutely scowled at *me*. You *should* have put her in the carriage, I must say."

"He couldn't!" interrupted Picard: "because I did; and two people can't perform that office unless they make a queen's cushion!"

"Oh, indeed!" said Miss Kate. "I suppose you think you'd do quite as well as Sir Henry. Not a bit of you. He's A 1 with the ladies. Haven't you found that out in all your travels? Why the *young* woman looked as if she'd eat poor *me*, when I only bowed to him! I mean the pale girl in a—— Gracious! Captain Vanguard, if you like me tell me so, or, at least, if you kick me under the table—don't kick so precious hard!"

"That was my daughter, Miss Kate," said Sir Henry, in perfect good-humour, interpreting very correctly Frank's too strenuous warning below the surface.

Kate got out of her difficulty gracefully enough.

"Your daughter!" she repeated "And a very nice daughter too. How fond she must be of you! I should, I know!"

Here Miss Cremorne exchanged glances with Vanguard, and Sir Henry felt a vague uncomfortable consciousness that the society was too young for him; relieved, however, by virtuous disapproval of Frank's promiscuous intimacies, and a dawning conviction that, if there had ever been any tendency to such an arrangement, he was well out of him for a son-in-law.

The sculptor now produced a velvet case of cigarettes which was handed round, and from which even the ladies did not disdain to take a few whiffs of the most fragrant tobacco in the world: Kilgarron only asking leave to indulge in a long strong Havanna, or "roofer," as he called it,—urging that to offer a man a cigarette when he wanted a cigar, was like giving him a slice of bread and butter when he asked for a beef-steak!

"Nonsense!" argued Mrs. Battersea. "Half

a loaf is better than no bread, and half a frolic than no fun,—consequently, half a puff is better than no smoke. What do *you* say, Kate? That's your second cigarette already."

The girl would have made a pretty picture, leaning back on the red velvet cushion of a sofa to which she had now betaken herself, while daintily holding the cigarette between her delicate fingers, she pursed up the rosiest and most provoking mouth imaginable to emit a long thin stream of aromatic smoke.

"What do I say?" she repeated, looking meaningly at Frank Vanguard. "That I hate half-loaves, half-frolics, half-mouthfuls, half-measures in *everything!* All or none, say I. Take it or let it alone!"

The foreign-looking woman tapped her snuff-box. "You're wrong," said she. "Everything in life is a matter of compromise. Besides, on *your* principle, my dear, you'd have all your eggs in one basket. Suppose you drop it?"

"What a mess there would be in the basket!" observed the sculptor.

"They'd make an omelette *annyhow,*" said Lord Kilgarron, mixing himself a brandy-and-soda at the side-board.

"Besides, there are fresh ones laid every day," added Picard.

"With chickens in them," continued Mrs. Battersea, "if you'll only have patience."

"And after all, one egg is very like another," murmured Sir Henry somewhat hazily; "dress them how you please, there's generally a suspicion about them, and the freshest are rather tasteless at their best."

Frank said nothing; but thought of the eggs he had most valued in the world, their basket, and its fate. Well, he had learned his lesson now. He must make the most of a pretty painted egg he had chosen to-night, from the shelf, indeed, rather than the nest, and must abide by his selection, defying memory, prudence, common sense—defying even the bright eyes, pleasant smiles, and winning whispers of Kate Cremorne.

A man who has lost the flower he values most

is perhaps never so unhappy as when he roams the garden to find a hundred others ready to be gathered, as sweet, as bright, as blooming, lacking only the subtle, special fragrance that was all in all to *him*. He is far less lonely in the desert than in that bower of beauty, which the absence of his rose—be she red, white, or yellow—has converted to a bare and dreary waste. Young hearts are sadly impatient of sorrow. Like young horses first put in harness, they are given to fret and bounce, and dash at any distraction which serves to divert their thoughts from the collar and the curb. Frank felt in no mood for self-communing to-night; but he was well disposed to snatch at any gratification the hour could afford. As the champagne mounted to his brain, Helen's pale, proud image faded into distance, and Jin's black eyes seemed to chain him in their spells. Ere long, he began to think he was a very lucky fellow after all, and exchanged jest or repartee with Kate Cremorne, as if he had not a care nor a sorrow in the world. That discriminating young person detected, nevertheless, something hollow in all this merriment.

"His heart's not in the game," she whispered to her sister, as the whole party took up a fresh position in the conservatory. "Something's gone wrong with Frank; and I think we needn't ask him to Greenwich next Sunday."

Henceforth she divided her smiles between the sculptor, whom she had known from her childhood, and Picard, on whom she bestowed perhaps the larger share, appreciating, as women do, a certain spice of the adventurer, which he betrayed, without parading, in dress, manner, gestures, even in the curl of his moustache, and the turn of his well-shaped, sinewy, sunburnt hands.

Sir Henry fell to Mrs. Battersea, who encouraged him to drink more champagne than is good for anybody after one in the morning; while Frank, placidly smoking, suffered himself to be amused by the foreign-looking Englishwoman, whose spirits seemed rather to increase than diminish with the waning hours.

So the night wore on. It was already four o'clock in a bright summer sunrise, when Sir Henry lighting a fresh cigar as he grappled to Picard's offered arm with great good-will—expressed his intention of walking home.

"Every yard of the way, my dear fellow. Does one all the good in the world. Nothing like exercise. Never had gout, though I'm bred for it both sides; and, faith, I've earned it, too! We used to live hard in my early days. But I always took a deal of exercise—always. That is why I'm pretty fresh on my legs now."

Picard assented, as younger men are bound to assent to such platitudes from their elders; and Sir Henry, whose pedestrianism was indeed of an exceedingly intermittent nature, puffed a volume of smoke in the rosy face of morning, and proceeded with his reflections.

"Now, Frank and that heavy fellow have gone off together on the chance of finding a cab. Much better have footed it like you and me. 'Gad, what a lovely day it's going to be! And what a pleasant night we've had! I'm not sure, though,"—here he turned round full on his companion—"I'm not sure we make the most of our lives after all. Hang it! if I had to begin again, I think I'd go in more for nature. Keep always out of doors, farm more, shoot more—look after the poor, hunt the country, and never go from home. I'm getting on now, and begin to understand the old Tartar chief, who longed for the Land of Grass when he was dying—

"And I would I were back in Cauca-land,
To hear my herdsmen's horn;
And to watch the waggons and brown brood mares,
And the tents where I was born!"

Picard had never read Kingsley's stirring verses. "This old chap's very drunk!" he thought; but having his own reasons for wishing to stand well with Miss Hallaton's father, he "hardened him on," as he would have called it, without remorse. "I don't think *you* can complain, Sir Henry," said he. "You've had the best of everything all your time, and can give pounds of weight to most of the young ones still. You might marry any woman in

London to-morrow if you liked. I wonder you don't."

Sir Henry looked pleased.

"Marry!" he repeated. "Marry! I'm not sure that I wouldn't, only, between you and me, my dear fellow, women in general are a very inferior lot. They're delightful, I grant you, wholesale; but when you come to the retail business, as the tradesmen say, there's great risk and very little profit about the article. They don't wear well when you buy, and if you want to sell, there's no market that I know of nearer than Constantinople. I fancy the Turks understand the business; but I am *not* a Turk. Heaven forbid! Fancy a plurality of wives!"

"I'm not sure I should mind it!" laughed Picard—"with the Bosphorus at one's door, of course."

"The Bosphorus wouldn't help you," said Sir Henry. "She'd come up again if she wanted, you may depend, though you sank her forty fathom deep, with a round-shot tied to her ankles. No; I think I understand the sex thoroughly. In my own experience, I've found them perverse, wilful, obstinate."

"Unselfish, at least," put in Picard.

"Unselfish!" exclaimed the other. "Not a bit of it! They're twice as selfish as we are, and that's saying a good deal. A tyrant, indeed, keeps them down, and so long as he remains perfectly unfeeling, the thing works moderately well. But if they can get what you and I call a good fellow to marry them, why he leads the life of a galley slave! There was my poor brother Ralph—I do believe, sir, he died of it—married a pig-headed idiot without two ideas, and she traded on his kind heart till she wore it clean away. I argued the point with her once. Fancy *arguing* with a woman, and an ignorant one! 'What should *you* say,' I asked, 'if Ralph took you out partridge-shooting, we'll suppose, and kept you for hours standing in wet turnips to load for him, or carry a spare gun? Yet you have no scruple in making him accompany you to parties, which he hates far more than you would the wet turnips, and are not ashamed to speak very unkindly to him even if he *looks* bored.' 'That's nothing to do with it,' she answered.—Such is a woman's logic.—'I daresay *you* wouldn't stand it; but then you've more character than Ralph!' She's married a stock-jobber since. I'm happy to say he bullies her like the devil, yet I do believe she likes him twice as well as Ralph."

"But *you* took warning, I hope, Sir Henry," said Picard, laughing in his sleeve.

"They never tried that sort of thing with *me*," answered the baronet. "Still there's no certainty about the thing, and I fancy it's better to let it alone. Besides, one's ideas vary about women in a regular procession of decades. Up to ten, we're dependent on them; from ten to twenty, we despise them; from twenty to thirty, we adore them; from thirty to forty, we believe in them; from forty to fifty, we mistrust them; from fifty to sixty, we avoid them; from sixty to seventy, we tolerate them; and if we live any longer after that, why we become dependent on them again."

Picard burst out laughing.

"A moral lesson!" he exclaimed, "and from one who has not neglected practice in theory. Here we are at your own door, Sir Henry. I shall not forget your maxims. Good night."

The other feeling for his latch-key, looked up where the blinds were drawn over the windows of Helen's bed-chamber.

"There are exceptions," said he musingly, "and one good one is worth all the others put together; and yet nine-tenths of our annoyances, and all our sorrows, can generally be traced to a woman."

Picard sighed as he turned away. Men may rail as they will, but each has a secret image of his own that he esteems a pearl of exceptional price, an angel far above the common shortcomings of humanity. Like the negro with his fetish, he takes it out sometimes to blame and scold, no less than plead with and adore, but he always puts it back reverently in its place, to nestle in the warmest and most sacred corner of his heart.

CHAPTER XIX.

A DRAWN BATTLE.

Mrs. Lascelles, retiring for the night, or rather morning, on her return from the Opera, found herself beset with troubles and perplexities of unusual gravity. Taking off her ornaments, and laying them one by one on the dressing-table, she reflected sadly on the relative positions of her two greatest friends, Jin Ross and Helen Hallaton. The longer she looked at the complication the less she liked it. For a woman to entertain two lovers, as a game-keeper hunts a brace of pointers, she considered natural enough. They should be made to range in different directions at her bidding, back each other without hesitation on her behalf, and, above all, come meekly to heel at the shortest notice when desired. This seemed only the normal condition of humanity, and, in her own case, she had hitherto found such amicable arrangements answer remarkably well. Sir Henry, indeed, proved wilder than any she had hitherto endeavoured to train; but Goldthred, again, if not the most sagacious, was by far the meekest and most docile she had ever taken in hand. For a moment, she laid down her brushes, smiled at her own comely face in the glass, and by some unaccountable association of ideas, found herself wishing this last admirer would show a little more self-assertion, more enterprise, altogether borrow a leaf or two out of the black books studied over-diligently by the former.

Then she reproached herself for giving a thought to her own concerns, while Helen Hallaton looked so pale and sad, resuming the thread of her regrets with the use of her hair-brushes, and cherishing a certain impulse of womanly indignation at the idea of two young ladies being in love with one man.

The proverb affirming that "What is sauce for the goose is sauce for the gander," cannot assuredly be of feminine invention. The code of our fair aggressors seems framed by a justice whose scales are not duly registered, and whose bandage does not entirely cover both eyes. "If I kill *you*," seems the ladies' verdict, "justifiable homicide, and it serves you right! But if you kill *me*, it's premeditated woman-slaughter, and penal servitude for life!"

How many of us are thus transported, without really deserving it, I refrain from speculating; but I am informed by convicts themselves that good conduct is powerless to obtain any remission of sentence, and that there is no such thing as a ticket-of-leave.

Before Mrs. Lascelles got into bed, she resolved to make a touching appeal to Jin's generosity directly after breakfast, and if need were, to back it with all the force of her own authority and moral influence.

"Moral influence!" the phrase carried with it a weight and dignity of which she herself felt conscious, even in bed; and must be overwhelming, she thought, to "dear Jin," who owed so much to their friendship, and who had not a bad disposition after all, though too reckless, and dreadfully wedded to her own opinion, right or wrong.

Turning her back on a ridiculous little night-light, utterly useless now that morning was already streaming through heavy curtains and close-drawn window-blinds, she became more and more impressed with the difficulty of her task, as she courted sleep in vain. So many instances recurred to her of Jin's superiority in argument, of Jin's readiness in repartee, of Jin's independence of spirit and inflexible persistency in taking her own line, that she was fain to dismiss the subject from her mind, and let her thoughts wander at will through more congenial topics—her dresses, her beauty, her widowhood, her rich brown hair, the Opera, the fiddles, the conductor's gloves, the tenor's eye-brows, Goldthred's good night, Sir Henry's back, a haze of lights, music, attentions, admiration, whiskers, boots and broadcloth, fading dimly into chaos, till they left Mrs. Lascelles fast asleep.

Miss Ross, too, laid her black head on the pillow with a sensation at her heart, so new, so strange, that it took away her breath—not triumph, for it was mingled with apprehension, misgivings, and a sense of unworthiness, as humiliating as it was unexpected;—not content, for everything seemed still to gain, except the one step made to-night, that yet to lose would be simply destruction and despair;—not happiness, surely, the uncertainty was even now too painful, the rush of joy too wild and keen. How useless, how idiotic it seemed, above all, how contemptible and unlike herself, to lock the door when she reached her room, rest her brow against the window-frame, and cry for two whole minutes like a child!

"Not for sorrow, though. Certainly not for sorrow," she murmured, recovering herself with a great sob, while she resolved to yield to such absurdity no longer.

She could hardly bring herself to believe in

the reality of the last few hours. The whole thing seemed wild and improbable as a dream. It was dreadful to think she might wake up at any moment, to discover that she had *not* known Captain Vanguard for a few weeks; that she had *not* set her heart on him, during the last few days, till he had become the one necessity of her existence; that she had *not* sat by his side this very evening in the gloomy back of an opera-box, and leant on his arm in the crush-room, and gathered from his looks, his gestures, nay, from his very words, that he loved her. *Her*, the outcast, the adventurer, the woman warring and warred against, who had vowed vengeance for her wrongs, on the whole of his base and treacherous sex. Ah! if she were indeed to wake and find so cold a reality awaiting her, would it not be better to end it all and go to sleep for ever? No; like a ray of light through a cloud, like a breath of air in the noon-day heat, like the song of a bird in a desert-place, came the recollection of her boy. What had she done to be so blessed? To have found her child, to have found her heart, to have found, even at the same moment, the love that makes a woman humble, and the love that makes a woman proud! It seemed too much, and, for a space, Jin was so happy that she felt almost good.

In such a frame of mind people's slumbers are light and easily disturbed. Long before the maid came in to call her, Miss Ross was wide-awake, and shaping for herself a plan, to be facilitated, and even rendered necessary, by subsequent events.

Breakfast at No. 40 was a late and unpunctual meal. It was laid in the boudoir, and each lady dawdling into that apartment at her own time, rang independently for the strip of dry toast and cup of coffee that constituted her repast. Miss Ross, earlier than usual, was surprised to find her hostess already down, making pretence of breakfasting, with obvious want of appetite, and a restlessness of manner denoting that uncomfortable state of mind which the sufferer calls "worry," and the bystander "fuss."

Jin entered radiant. Fresh from her bath and morning toilet, she had even a tinge of colour in her cheek, the one thing usually wanting to complete her beauty. There was a light, too, dancing in her eyes, a buoyancy in her step and gesture, a sparkle, as it were, of joy and triumph in her whole bearing, that did not escape the notice of her friend.

Late hours seem to suit you, my dear," said Mrs. Lascelles languidly. "I never saw you looking so well."

"I am a fool about music," answered the other demurely, "and I did enjoy the opera last night more than I can describe."

"The opera," asked Mrs. Lascelles quietly, "or the company?"

Jin must have been hard hit, for she actually blushed.

"Both, of course," was her reply. "Everything is pleasanter, I suppose, when it's done with pleasant people."

The tone was rather too careless, and her hand shook while she poured out a cup of coffee. Mrs.

Lascelles, noticing this trepidation, felt her heart sink within her.

"The company was pleasant enough last night," said she, "as far as *our* box was concerned; but I don't think people all amused themselves equally. Helen, for instance, seemed bored to death. She does *not* look well, and I'm sure she is not happy. I'm very fond of her, Jin, and so are you. What *is* it, do you think? and how can we do her good?"

These ladies were not fairly matched. Mrs. Lascelles became flurried and nervous as she neared the point of collision. Miss Ross, on the contrary, grew steadier and cooler with the immediate approach of danger.

"I don't think Helen knows her own mind," she replied; "girls very seldom do. You must surely have observed in your personal experience, Rose, that—

"Too many lovers will puzzle a maid."

Mrs. Lascelles accepted the implied compliment with a forced smile, but it did not turn her from her object.

"Helen is unlike most girls," she answered; "and I don't fancy any number of lovers would make amends to her for losing the one she has set her heart on. People are so different, you know, and Helen's is one of those deep, quiet, reserved natures, that suffer awfully, though they suffer in silence. I think, Jin, between you and me, that Helen likes Somebody, and that Somebody would like her if it wasn't for Somebody else!"

Though almost sublime in its ambiguity, Miss Ross understood this "dark sentence" perfectly, and scorned to affect misconception of its purport.

"You mean Captain Vanguard!" She came out with his name in a burst of defiance. "Well, how can I help *that?*"

"Oh, Jin, as you are strong be merciful!" pleaded Mrs. Lascelles. "You know your own power. You know you are one of the most taking creatures in the world if you only try. Look at Uncle Joseph, look at even Mr. Goldthred, though I consider him the truest of the true. Look at Sir Henry. To be sure, it's no compliment from *him*, for he's the same to everybody. Look at all the men who come near us. You needn't even take the trouble of shooting, like Mr. Picard's American colonel and his squirrel—down they come at once. Can't you let this squirrel alone? Can't you leave him to Helen, dear? Everybody will be so pleased, and I should be *so* much obliged to you, Jin, if you would!"

Miss Ross laughed. "The last is certainly a strong inducement," said she; "but it seems to me you are leaving the squirrel's own inclinations out of the question. Because he comes down for Colonel Crockett, does it follow he'll be so obliging to everybody else? I suppose Frank—I mean Captain Vanguard—has a perfect right to talk to me instead of Miss Hallaton, if he is more amused in my society than in hers."

"Amused!" repeated Mrs. Lascelles, growing warm. "This is no question of amusement. It is a life's happiness or misery for two people who ought never to have been interfered with. You have no right to supplant her; you have no right to trifle with *him!*"

"Suppose I am *not* trifling," retorted the other. "Suppose I am in earnest, just for once, by way of change. You have complimented me on my powers, in sport. Do you think I should be a less dangerous enemy, Rose, if I were fighting for my life?"

"You remember our agreement," exclaimed Mrs. Lascelles with rising colour, and a shake in her voice, denoting wrath no less than a nervous dread of its indulgence. "You are not acting fairly by me; you're not acting fairly by any of us. If you turn round now, after what you've told me, after what we agreed, I can never trust you again, Jin. I shall think you've been sailing under false colours all through."

"Explain yourself, Rose," said Miss Ross, very quietly, but with an ominously steady expression about the lower part of her face, in strong contrast with the quivering lips and tremulous chin of her companion.

"You ought to see it yourself," whimpered the latter, now in a sore predicament between her feelings of friendship and generosity. "I shall say something to be sorry for afterwards. I know I shall. You'll drive me to it, Jin; and when I am driven, I can't and won't stop!"

"You seem to expect that my thoughts, feelings, and opinions are to be under your control, as you would have my actions and conversation," was the grave and rather stern rejoinder. "This is not dependence, Mrs. Lascelles, but slavery. You are not only unkind, but unreasonable and unjust."

Mrs. Lascelles turned very red. She was now obviously "driven," as she called it, and not likely to stop.

"What I expect," she retorted, "is nothing to the purpose; for there seems little chance of my obtaining it. What I *insist* on is common propriety of demeanour and the merest fair-play. You would never have met these people at all—you would never have been in a position to know any one of them, but for *me*. You are received amongst them as—as—like anybody else, and you throw down the apple of discord to set us all at sixes and sevens. You seem to forget, Miss Ross, that your victims are my personal friends."

"And what am I?" retorted Jin, with an angry flash from her black eyes. "Something between a companion and a servant! A piece of furniture good enough for the drawing-room, though occasionally useful in the kitchen! The obligations are not perhaps so entirely on one side as you would like to make out. When people hunt in couples, a good deal may be done that it would be madness to attempt singly. It cannot but be convenient for an independent lady to have a friend at her elbow who is always well disposed, always ready to go anywhere, or do anything, generally good-tempered, and, above all, afflicted with an intermittent defect of sight or hearing as required. I think I have earned my wages, and returned adequate value in kind for board and lodging—both, I must admit of the best—and treatment, I am happy to think, of the kindest and most considerate, till to-day!"

Touched to the quick by this last reproach, Mrs. Lascelles was already crying vehemently.

"It's not that!" she sobbed out. "It's not that! I don't want to remind you of anything that's past and gone. But you ought to do what I ask you in common gratitude, because—because—you know you ought!"

Seeing the adversary wavering, Miss Ross stood firm to her guns.

"Gratitude," said she, "is one thing, and obedience another. I admit that I owe the first, and hoped I had shown some consciousness of the debt. The last is a different question, and I am not naturally very submissive. But, come. Let us have a clear understanding. I am ready to receive your orders."

"Orders!" Mrs. Lascelles fired up once more. "You've no right to put it in that way. But it's no use talking the thing over backwards and forwards. You've barely known him a fortnight. In plain English, will you or will you *not* give Frank Vanguard up?"

Jin laughed scornfully.

"Suppose he won't give *me* up?"

"That's nothing to do with it," retorted the other. "Once for all, Miss Ross, will you, or will you *not?*"

"No, I won't! There!"

Jin looked very handsome while she thus raised the standard of revolt, with her head up, her eyes flashing, and a little spot of colour in each cheek.

Mrs. Lascelles now lost all control over her temper. Totally unused to anger, she trembled violently under its influence, and felt, indeed, that no victory, however triumphant, could repay her for the tumult of such a contest.

"Under these circumstances," said she, vainly endeavouring to steady her voice, and assume that dignity of bearing to which only last night her "moral influence" had seemed to entitle her, "it is impossible that you and I can continue on the same terms. It is impossible that we can remain under the same roof. You will see the propriety, Miss Ross, at your earliest convenience of making arrangements to reside elsewhere."

"The sooner the better," answered Jin calmly. "I'll go directly. My things are packed. We won't part in anger, Mrs. Lascelles. Rose, you've been very, *very* good to me, and I shall think kindly of you as long as I live!"

The tide of battle was now completely turned. It may be that the conqueror was eagerly looking for an opportunity to lay down her arms—it may be that Mrs. Lascelles had only meant to threaten, and hated herself for the menace even while it crossed her lips. She was, at any rate, quite incapable of hitting an adversary when down, and far more inclined to set a fallen foe upright, and make friends, than, like some Amazons, to crush and trample the unfortunate into the dust. She literally fell on Miss Ross's neck, and wept.

"I didn't mean it!" she sobbed. "I didn't mean it! Jin, dear Jin, I was angry, and didn't know what I was saying! I am a wretch and a heathen and a beast! Think no more of it, dear, I implore you! And promise me that you won't dream of packing up your things and leaving me. What should I do without you, Jin? Indeed—indeed—I should be perfectly miserable, dear, if you were to go away!"

So the ladies embraced, and cried, and laughed, and cried again, as is the manner of their sex in the ratification of all treaties, permanent or otherwise, arriving at the conclusion that their friendship was imperishable, that they were all in all to each other, and that henceforth nothing should part them but the grave. None the less, however, did Miss Ross determine that she would subject herself no more to such scenes of reproach and recrimination; that she would take a certain step, only, after all, a little sooner than expected, which she had already vaguely contemplated as a possibility, a probability, nay, a positive necessity, for her happiness; and, if he would only open them to receive her, throw herself, without delay, into the arms of Frank Vanguard.

CHAPTER XX.

A RECONNAISANCE.

VIOLENT tempests like that described in the last chapter do not pass away without leaving a "ground swell," as it were, on the domestic surface. Neither Mrs. Lascelles nor Miss Ross felt disposed to take their usual drive in the open carriage for the purpose of shopping and "leaving cards;" two functions that constitute the whole duty of women, from three to six p.m. of every week-day, during the London season. The principle of acquisitiveness inherent in the female breast, together with an insatiable desire to see and to be seen, may account for the shopping; but why society enjoins the penance of leaving cards surpasses my comprehension altogether. Unmeaning, endless, and exceedingly troublesome, this custom seems to produce no definite result, but to fill the waste-paper basket with a multitude of other cards left in return. To-day, however, the ladies at No. 40 resolved they would devote their afternoon to refreshment and repose: a good luncheon, a comfortable arm-chair, the newest novel, and a casual dropping in of visitors to tea.

The luncheon was heavy, the arm-chair provocative of slumbers; so was the novel; and Mrs. Lascelles, I am bound to admit, went fast asleep over its pages; while Miss Ross stole softly upstairs to read one important little note, write another, and otherwise bring her schemes to maturity.

In the meantime, a considerable bustle was going on in Messrs. Tattersalls' celebrated emporium for the sale of horses—good, bad, and indifferent. To use correct language, "The entire stud of a nobleman, well known in Leicestershire," was being brought to the hammer; and a very motley crowd of sportsmen, dandies, horse-dealers, lords, louts, yeomen, yokels, and nondescripts were gathered round the auctioneer's box in consequence. A well-bred chestnut horse, with magnificent shoulders, and a white fore-leg, was the object of competition at the moment Sir Henry Hallaton entered the yard; and, although he neither wanted a hunter, nor could have afforded to buy this one even at its reserved price, it was not in his power to refrain from elbowing his way through the crowd, and stationing himself in perilous vicinity to the hind-legs of the animal.

"Handsome—fast—up to great weight—with an European reputation! And only two hundred bid for him!" said the voice of Fate from under an exceedingly well-brushed and rather curly-brimmed hat; while the object of these encomiums, whose restless eye and ear denoted excitement, if not alarm, gave a stamp of his foot and a whisk of his tail that caused considerable swaying, surging, and treading on toes in the encircling crowd.

"Ten! Twenty!" continued the voice of Fate. "Thirty! Thank you, my lord. Fifty!

Two hundred and fifty bid for him. Run him down once more. Take care!" And Sir Henry found himself jostled against his new friend Picard, who, having made the last bid with an assumption of great carelessness, seemed in danger of becoming the actual proprietor of this desirable purchase.

"Make me a wheeler, I think," said he, as the horse was led back to the stable, and another brought out to elicit a fresh burst of competition, all the more lively, perhaps, that the Leicestershire nobleman had put such a reserve price on his stud as precluded the sale of anything but a hack he didn't like.

"Rather light for harness," observed Sir Henry, with a certain covert approval of his friend's extravagance. "I suppose they *are* to be sold?" he added, on further reflection.

"I conclude so, of course," replied the other, though he well knew they were *not*, and had been bidding pompously for some half-dozen with the comfortable conviction that there was nothing to pay for his whistle.

"It's a long price," resumed the baronet, as he took Picard's arm to saunter leisurely in the direction of Belgravia. "At least, it makes them very dear when you come to match them. That's the worst of having too good a team."

"Oh! I don't know," said Picard loftily. "I always find it cheapest, in the long run, to drive the best horses, though I do have to give thundering prices now and then, I admit. Still, things must begin to look up for us soon. We Southern proprietors can't be always on the shady side of the hedge; and we've had a rough time of it enough, in all conscience."

They were already at the gate, and it appeared this "Southern proprietor" had no intention of buying any more horses to-day.

Sir Henry hazarded a pertinent, or, as he himself considered it, an *im*pertinent, inquiry.

"Have you much property," said he, "in the South? And do you get anything from it?"

"Not, perhaps, what *you* would call much, in actual value," answered his companion; "but for extent, of course, unlimited." He waved his arm as Robinson Crusoe might, while describing his circle

> "From the centre all round to the sea."

"But American property," he added, "is so difficult to define. Halloo! here's our friend Vanguard."

That gentleman was indeed strolling leisurely into the yard, apparently with no particular object, for he strolled out again willingly enough at the invitation of his two friends.

"It's rather early for the park," observed Picard, as the three crossed to the shady side of the street, "and too late for St. James's Street. What shall we do with ourselves for the next half hour?"

"Go and look at the Serpentine—see if it's still there," said Frank, who seemed in unusually high spirits, though his manner was somewhat restless. "If that bores you, there's always the British Museum. It's cool, and, I've been told, very solitary."

"Too far off," answered Sir Henry, in perfect good faith. "No. I'll tell you what. Let's go and ask Mrs. Lascelles to give us a cup of tea."

Frank started, and his heart thumped against a little note lying in his waistcoat-pocket; but, though the thump was for Helen, the note was from some one very different to that well-conducted young lady. Was he disloyal enough, even now, to leap at the chance of seeing Miss Hallaton just once more, and for the last time? If so, he was doomed to be disappointed, and it served him right.

Picard, who carried no notes of any description in his pockets, and whose heart seldom beat unless he walked fast up-hill, agreed willingly to the baronet's proposition. He, too, entertained a vague sentiment of admiration for Helen, capable of soon ripening into something warmer if she had any fortune, and under such circumstances his game now was to see as much of her as he could.

Thus it fell out, that these three gentlemen, arriving at Mrs. Lascelles's door, found themselves face to face with Uncle Joseph, fresh from the City, who had just rung the bell, and was utilising his time by grinding a pair of thick soles fiercely against the scraper.

It would have amused a bystander to observe the effect produced on each visitor by the footman's appearance and the information he tendered.

"Has Miss Hallaton been here?" said Sir Henry, whose position on the top step gave him priority of speech with the door-keeper.

"Called to leave a note after luncheon, Sir Henry, and I was to say she'd' a-gone out driving with Lady Sycamore, and wouldn't be home till seven, if you came for her here."

Picard, pulling out a memorandum-book, muttered that "he had forgotten an appointment at his Club," while Frank's face darkened, and he smothered something between an oath and a sigh.

"Is Miss Ross at home?" then demanded Uncle Joseph, with the air of a man who submits to an unnecessary formality in compliance with the usages of society.

"Miss Ross had stepped out—oh! *not* five minutes ago—the gentlemen might almost have met her at the corner of the street."

Frank now seemed uneasy, looked at his watch, observed it was "rather too late to call," and disappeared.

Uncle Joseph gasped. Did Miss Ross leave no message? For *him*, Mr. Groves? Was the man quite sure?

The man *was* quite sure, so far as he knew; should he ask the maid?

"D——n the maid!" I am sorry to say, was Uncle Joseph's reply, and without further leave-taking he bustled off in a towering passion, while Sir Henry and the footman, on the door-step, contemplated each other in some amusement and no little surprise.

The baronet broke into a laugh.

"You soon clear off your visitors, James. Is Mrs. Lascelles at home to *me!*"

"Certainly, sir! Yes, sir. In the boodore, sir!" answered James. "I'd just taken in tea when you rang."

So Sir Henry found himself *tête-à-tête* with the lady for whom, during the foregoing winter, he had half-felt and half-professed a spurious kind of attachment, and was conscious of an uncomfortable wish that he, too, had made his escape with the others, or that it had never entered his head to come to tea at all.

She was always gracious, just as she was always well-dressed. There is a dignity and a decency of beauty, which nothing will induce a beautiful woman to forego. It was a very cool and steady hand that Mrs. Lascelles tendered to her vacillating admirer, while she bade him sit down, and poured him out a cup of tea.

"I was on the point of writing to you," said she; "but you have saved me the trouble. I wanted to see you, Sir Henry, very much. I have something particular to say."

He bowed, and settled himself in a low easy-chair with his back to the windows. No faded beauty of the other sex could have entertained a greater objection than Sir Henry to flourishing "crow's-feet" and wrinkles in the light of day.

"It's no wonder I'm here," was the smiling reply, "for I always want to see you!"

"And without anything particular to say,"

she retorted, adding hurriedly—"However, that's not the point. Sir Henry, you care for your daughter?"

"More than for anything in the world!" was his grave rejoinder.

"I know it—I know it," she answered, and the colour deepened in her cheek. "Well, now, men are blind as bats, I think, in all matters of affection; but have you not lately noticed an alteration in Helen's manner, spirits, in her very looks? Can't you see there's something wrong with the girl? Can't you guess what it is?"

He looked startled, disturbed, distressed.

"Not the lungs, Mrs. Lascelles!" he exclaimed. "She runs up-stairs like a lapwing, and will waltz for twenty minutes together at a spin. There can't be much amiss. Not her lungs, surely; nor her heart!"

Mrs. Lascelles laughed.

"Yes, her heart," she repeated, "though not in the sense *you* mean. Not anatomically, but sentimentally, I fear; which is sometimes almost as bad."

He looked immensely relieved.

"Oh! she'll get over that," said he, putting more sugar in his tea. "She's a sensible girl, Helen, with a good deal of self-respect, and what I should call 'mind.' No whims, no fancies, in any way, and not the least romantic."

"Like her papa," observed Mrs. Lascelles maliciously.

"I trust in heaven *not!*" he replied, with unusual energy. "Helen is as much my superior in intellect as she is in moral qualities. She has talent, energy, self-control, and self-denial; none of which, I fear, can she inherit from *me*. Her sincerity, too, and trustfulness are like a child's, and she is as fond of me now as she was at two years old. You don't think she *really* cares for anybody, do you, Mrs. Lascelles? It might be a serious thing for her if she did, and I had rather everything I have in the world went to ruin than that Helen should be made unhappy."

"I do," answered Mrs. Lascelles. "I think she cares for Frank Vanguard."

"Confound him!" ejaculated Sir Henry, upsetting his tea-cup. "A presuming young jack-ass! And not over steady, I'm afraid," he added, reverting in his own mind to certain memories connected with supper, cigarettes, champagne, three o'clock in the morning, and Kate Cremorne.

"Now that's so like a *man!*" said his hostess. "You want to keep your treasure all to yourself, and are furious with everybody who agrees with you in appreciating its value. Captain Vanguard is young, good-looking, a gentleman, and not badly off. Why shouldn't your daughter like him, and why shouldn't he like your daughter? Sir Henry, I needn't ask if you believe in my inclination, do you also believe in my ability to serve you?"

"Certainly," was the polite reply. "Nobody is half so clever, and, besides, you are a perfect woman of the world."

"Will you be guided by my advice?"

"What do you propose?" was the natural answer to so comprehensive a question.

"Get Helen out of town at once. Carry her

off to Windsor. I can take upon myself to offer you The Lilies. Uncle Joseph will lend the cottage to me, or any of my friends, for as long as I like. Give her plenty of amusement, but no dissipation. Early hours, a glass of port wine and a biscuit every day at twelve, and don't let her stay out after sun-down. In three weeks the girl will be in rude health, or I know nothing of a woman's constitution and ailments."

"But what has all this to do with Captain Vanguard?" asked Sir Henry, fixing in his mind, not without effort, the whole regimen, particularly the port wine at twelve o'clock.

"Oh! blindest of baronets!" laughed Mrs. Lascelles. "Lady Sycamore, or any other chaperon, would have seen it at once. Captain Vanguard is quartered at Windsor. Helen is staying at The Lilies. The young people meet every day. A mutual attachment, already, I firmly believe, in the bud, comes to maturity. General *tableau!* You give your blessing, and will become, I hope, more respectable as a father-in-law than you have hitherto been in other relations of life."

"I'll do anything for Helen—anything!" said Sir Henry vehemently. "And how can I thank you enough, Mrs. Lascelles, for your kindness and the interest you take in my girl? You'll come down every Saturday, and stay till Monday, to see how your prescription answers, of course?"

"Not the least of course," she replied. "Jin and I mean to take ourselves off to Brighton by the end of the week. If the fine weather lasts, we shall very likely go on to Dieppe."

This, then, was her kindly scheme: to get Miss Ross out of Frank Vanguard's way to leave the coast clear for Helen; and then, having settled matters to her own satisfaction, weigh Sir Henry deliberately against Goldthred, and take whichever she considered most deserving of herself.

Mrs. Lascelles never doubted her power over anyone on whom she chose to exert it, and believed that, like a spider, she need only spin her web in order to surround the desired bluebottle inextricably with its toils.

In hers, as in similar cases, I imagine that to break boldly through the meshes was the insect's best chance of turning the tables, and taking the custodian herself into custody.

"Miss Ross goes with you?" asked Sir Henry meditatively, though I believe he was thinking less of that black-eyed syren than of his daughter.

"Miss Ross goes with me, undoubtedly," was the answer, spoken rather sharply, and in some little displeasure. "Have you any objection? Can't you bear to part with her even for so short a period? You see, I know all about *that*, too."

Sir Henry never seemed to have any sense of shame. He couldn't have blushed to save his life. To this callousness he owed many of his successes, and almost all his scrapes.

He smiled pleasantly. "You know all about everything, I believe," said he; "and you *think* you know all about *me*. But you don't, and I don't; and nobody does, I fancy. I'm so different from what I feel sure I was intended to be, that I sometimes suspect, like the Irishman, they 'changed me at nurse.' Only, if I *were* somebody else, that wouldn't account for it, after all, would it? These are puzzling speculations; but I know I *could* have been a better and a very different man. It's not my fault."

"Whose, then?" she asked, bending her blue eyes on him with an expression of interest extremely dangerous for a man at any age.

He scarcely marked it. He was searching out the truth for once from the depths—not very profound—of his world-worn heart, and had forgotten during the moment that false and fleeting woman-worship which had so weakened and deteriorated his nature. Looking back along the path of life on which, as in some idolatrous grove, his every step had been marked by a soulless image of brass, or stucco, or marble, reared only to be defaced and overthrown, he was scarcely conscious of that lovely living companion, listening with all the attention of curiosity and self-interest to his retrospections.

"Yours!" he answered—("Now it's coming," she thought)—"Yours! Not individually, but collectively, as of that sex which seems to be the natural bane of ours. If I could begin again, I would forswear female society altogether. I should be a better, and certainly a happier man. As it is, my life has been wasted in looking for something I always failed to find. Did you ever see Grantley Berkeley's book? There it is on the table. I daresay you've never looked into it. Read it, if you want to find poetry in sport. He seems to entertain a gentle, kindly feeling for every living creature, wild or tame. He tells a story of one of his hounds—Champion or Challenger, if I remember right--that used to detach itself from the pack on hunting mornings, and come to its mistress's pony-chaise for a morsel of biscuit and a caress. Ever afterwards, when drafted into another county, the faithful, true-hearted dog would break away, and gallop up to every open carriage that arrived at the meet, returning from each succeeding disappointment with a sadder expression on his wise, honest face—a more piteous look in his meek, brown, wistful eyes. I've been like poor Champion or Challenger. So often, I've thought I had found my heart's desire at last! Then I strained every nerve to win, and *did* win, too; only to learn, over and over again, that she had not deceived me half so deeply as I had deceived myself. Shall I confess that the woman who, in my whole life, has approached nearest the ideal of my heart, was one whom my reason, my experience, and my moral sense, deteriorated though it is, convicted as the vilest and the worst?"

Few people had ever seen Sir Henry in earnest. Certainly not Mrs. Lascelles; and she was almost frightened.

"Good gracious!" she exclaimed. "After such an experience, you'll surely never try again?"

He seemed to wake up from a dream. The ruling passion was not to be controlled; and habit, stronger than nature, impelled him, though for the hundredth time, to recommence the old story in the old, familiar strain.

"Just once more," he said, drawing his chair nearer the frail spider-legged tea-table that constituted the only barrier between them. "It's hard if a man seeks all his life without finding his object at last. Mrs. Lascelles, may I not say——"

In another moment she might have had the satisfaction of hearing, and perhaps repelling, a fervent declaration of attachment; but, at this juncture, the door of the boudoir was thrown open, and the announcement of "Lady Clearwell!" by James in person, ushered in an exceedingly courteous and sprightly personage, all smiles and rustle, who called Mrs. Lascelles "Rose," took her by both hands, and, with a distant bow to Sir Henry, dropped on the sofa as if she meant to make herself perfectly at home.

Such interruptions are almost a matter of course. There was nothing for it but to take up his hat and make his bow.

It may be that Sir Henry, walking soberly down-stairs, reflected, not without gratitude, how such little *contretemps* constitute the great charm and safeguard of society in general.

Lady Clearwell stayed till nearly seven. As her carriage rolled away, Mrs. Lascelles looked wistfully at the clock, and called over the banisters to James—

"I'm not at home to anybody *now*, except Mr. Goldthred."

But Mr. Goldthred never came.

CHAPTER XXI.

THE SOHO BAZAAR.

FRANK VANGUARD, leaving the threshold of No. 40 with unusual alacrity, lost no time in securing one of the many Hansom cabs that are to be found crawling about Belgravia, plentiful as wasps on wall-fruit, every summer's afternoon. "Soho Bazaar," said he. "Don't go to sleep over it!" And so found himself, in less than a quarter of an hour, at the door of that heterogeneous emporium. It did not seem to surprise him in the least, that, while he paid his driver, the well-known figure of Miss Ross should precede him into the building, nor that he should come upon her, minutely examining ornaments of bog-oak, at the very first counter which offered a secluded corner for confidential communication.

The place seemed well adapted for secrecy; purchasers, it appeared, there were none, while the sellers, women of various ages and costumes, were mostly nodding drowsily behind their wares.

Jin looked up from a clumsy black cross set in Irish diamonds, and her eyes flashed brighter than the spurious gems while, putting her hand in Frank's arm, she nestled to his side, as though henceforth her refuge was there alone.

"You got my note?" she whispered. "I didn't know what to do. My only chance was to see you at once, and I could think of no place so good as this."

"Dearest!" he murmured, pressing the arm that clung so fondly to his own, looking about him, nevertheless, in uncomfortable apprehension of observant bystanders, or sharp-sighted acquaintance.

"I have had such a battle to fight," she continued, leading him into a grove of waving drapery, consisting chiefly of clothing for young people. "If I hadn't *felt* I could depend upon you, I think I must have given way. I've behaved so badly to Mrs. Lascelles, so cruelly to Mr. Groves. I've done so wrong, by everybody but *you.*"

"Dearest!" he repeated, with another squeeze. His ideas were gradually deserting him, nor did he know exactly what he was expected to say in reply.

"They all wanted to persuade me," she continued. "They all wanted to talk me into it; and in my position, so completely friendless and forlorn, it would have been an excellent arrangement, of course—far the wisest thing to do. But I couldn't. No, I couldn't, when I thought of *you.*"

"I didn't quite make out from your note," said Frank, collecting his wits with some difficulty. "You wrote it in a hurry, I daresay. You mentioned something about old Groves. Had he—had he the impudence to ask you to marry him?"

She turned round with a comical expression of mingled pain and amusement in her face.

"Do you think it requires so much effrontery?" she demanded. "Recollect my position, or rather total want of it. Recollect that Mr. Groves is rich, amiable, kind-hearted, and, after all, not so *very* old, that is, for *a man*. Just the sort of person to make a good, trustworthy, affectionate husband."

"Then why didn't you take him?" said Frank; but the tone of pique in which he spoke, told Miss Ross the game was in her own hand.

She let go his arm, looking reproachfully into his very eyes.

"Can *you* ask me, Captain Vanguard?" she exclaimed, in sorrowful accents, stopping short under a pair of elaborate blue knickerbockers, ticketed seven-and-nine. "If so, I have indeed acted madly in meeting you here to-day. No; let go my hand. Before I walk a step farther tell me if you really mean what you say!"

"You know what I mean," he answered, in an agitated whisper. "You know that you are everything in the world to *me*. That if you took up with any other fellow you would drive me mad, and that I would rather we were both in our graves than you should marry such a 'guy' as old Groves!"

They were pacing on through the bazaar once more, Frank having re-possessed himself of his companion's arm, while he made the foregoing statement, with every appearance of earnestness and truth.

Jin stopped short at a counter, on which were displayed a variety of children's toys in gaudy profusion.

"What a love!" she exclaimed, pouncing on a parti-coloured little figure-of-fun with bells at all its angles. "Twelve-and-sixpence? Put it up for me, please, Captain Vanguard; don't look so astonished. It's only a plaything for my boy!"

Frank's eyes opened wide; perhaps for that reason his ears failed to detect something forced and embarrassed in the laugh with which Miss Ross greeted his surprise.

"I have no secrets from you *now*," she continued. "You and I must trust each other entirely, or not at all. I have never told you about my boy, but I cannot and will not give him up, even for you, Frank. Take me with my encumbrances, or not at all. *C'est tout simple!*" Watching his looks as the steersman watches a coming wave, something warned her to avoid the imminent shock. Like a skilful pilot, she luffed, so to speak, several points to the windward of truth.

"He has nobody else to depend on in the world," she said, eyeing Frank's face with a touching and plaintive gaze. "People blame me, I daresay, but I know I'm doing right, for after all, is he not my own sister's child?"

Frank drew a long breath, looking immensely relieved, yet conscious the while of a vague perception, not entirely agreeable, that the last link in his fetters was about to be riveted for good and all.

"You're an angel," said he—"a real angel, I do believe. I begin to see it more every day. At first, I used to think you could be very wicked if you chose. Tell me all about it. I know you will tell me the——"

He could not have believed those slender fingers were strong enough to inflict such a grip as at this moment interrupted his sentence, and hurried him on to a different part of the bazaar so rapidly as to entail no small risk of upsetting many fragile articles exposed for sale at the corners of the different stalls; not, however, before he was aware of an exceedingly frigid bow from Lady Shuttlecock, a stare of unbounded astonishment from at least two of her daughters, and a wink of intense amusement from Kilgarron, who, surrounded by children of all sizes, was obviously in attendance on aunt, cousins, and relations of every degree.

This numerous family-party did not affect to conceal their surprise at Frank's appearance in such an unlikely place and with so charming a companion. Had the pair walked boldly up to Lady Shuttlecock to exchange with these new arrivals the customary greetings of people who see each other much oftener than they desire, it would probably have been inferred that Mrs. Lascelles was shopping in some other part of the building, and no further notice would have been taken of the circumstance; but Jin's sudden flight, the result perhaps of studied calculation, was compromising in the last degree, and her ladyship, gathering her brood around her, began to fan herself with a vigour of disapproval not calculated to cool an exuberant matron in the dog-days. As her head, rising inch by inch, attained the level from which propriety looks down on indiscretion, she turned fiercely to Kilgarron, and observed, as if it was *his* fault—

"Most extraordinary! *Your* friend Captain Vanguard and, of all people in the world, Miss Ross!"

"It couldn't have been Miss Ross, mamma," interposed Lady Selina in sprightly innocence. "She never would have run away from us as if we'd got the plague."

"Nonsense, Selina," said her sister. "She was ashamed of herself, and well she might be.

I always thought her an odious person; and as for *your* friend, Kil, I don't believe he's much better."

"Bother!" replied Kilgarron. "She's his cousin, sure! Mayn't a man take his cousin to the Soho Bazaar, and buy fairings for her? Never say it! I'll be emptying the counter here for mine this minute!"

So popular a declaration was received by the young fry with acclamations that reached the ears of Frank and Jin, who had retired for sanctuary to the loneliness of the picture-room.

"I am lost *now!*" exclaimed the latter, really out of breath from the pace at which they fled. "It will be all over London to-night. The girls hate me like poison. The mother's the greatest gossip in Europe. Lord Kilgarron will make a joke of it at the mess-table! Captain Vanguard —Frank—what is to become of me? Don't look so cross! What am I to do?"

He pondered. His face was very grave—almost, as she said, cross. Suddenly it lighted up, smiling fondly down into her own.

"There is a very easy way out of it," he said—"a way to stop all their mouths; but perhaps you wouldn't like it!"

"To marry Mr. Groves?" said she, with one of her most mischievous glances and her merriest laugh.

He laughed in concert.

"If you like, darling," he answered, "at some future time; but not whilst I'm alive. It's my turn first."

"Oh, Frank!" was all she said; and for a moment she felt she loved him too dearly to sacrifice him to such a fate.

But the temptation was overwhelming. So many considerations crowded on her brain: her state of dependence, now more than ever irksome since the late difference with Mrs. Lascelles; the awkwardness of meeting Uncle Joseph daily, and the impossibility of refusing to give him a decided answer; the equal impossibility, after all she had led him to expect, of saying anything but Yes; the delight—and this to one of her temperament and antecedents was not without considerable charm—of anything like an elopement or a clandestine marriage, not counting the triumph of carrying off such a prize as Frank Vanguard from the many women who would be too happy to make him their lawful prey; the impression—vague, unreasoning, and essentially feminine—that such a step would free her at once and for ever from any claim Picard might advance on her person, her belongings, or her child; finally—and it is only justice to insist that this was the strongest inducement of all—the undisturbed possession of that child, whom she resolved to carry off with her in her flight, but whose relationship to herself, it pained her to think, she must now disguise for evermore.

Vanguard, drawing her towards him, was surprised to find the tears running down her cheeks.

He didn't care if a hundred Lady Shuttlecocks were watching: he wound his arm round her waist, and she buried her face impulsively in his breast. For half a minute or so, they were both very much in earnest and very happy.

Then she looked up, and adjusted her bonnet with a smile.

"How shocked St. Sebastian will be!" she observed; that sparingly-clothed martyr, execrably painted, having indeed been the only witness of this improper ebullition.

"It must be done at once," said Frank; now that he was fairly in for it, characteristically keen and impatient of inaction. "You can't go back to No. 40. I won't have you persecuted by that old idiot, Groves. We ought to start from here, you and I, just as we are—swagger into the first church that we see—they're always open—and get it over."

She smiled very sweetly now on his impatience.

"You rash, inconsiderate darling!" she said. "That's impossible. I wish it wasn't. No. You shall be guided by me, and let me have my own way. In the first place, I must go back to No. 40 for many reasons. Well, if you insist on knowing, I must get some more things. I am very glad you like this dress; but it wouldn't do for one's whole outfit. Don't look so alarmed: my wardrobe is not very large, and I know where I can have it taken care of without dragging about with me more than I require. To-morrow I shall be free."

"And to-morrow I must be at Windsor—at least in the afternoon," observed Frank in an injured tone. "Why the colonel can't inspect my young horses without *me* I don't know. The whole lot are not worth five pounds. But I can get away by six o'clock."

"At Windsor!" repeated Jin. "The very thing! Now listen, Frank, and I will arrange it all in a way that will disarm suspicion, and leave no trace of us after we have made our escape. You shall go down to your barracks and attend to your duties, like a good boy. I mean you to be always subservient to discipline. When your colonel has done with you, it will be my turn. You will get into a skiff, or whatever you call it —a boat that has room enough for two people, and cushions, and all that—you shall row it to the very place I got in at—don't you remember—the day you saved my life? and—and you will find me waiting there. Take me or leave me; as I said before, Frank, I have nobody in the world now but you."

He lifted her hand passionately to his lips. "Take you!" he repeated, "I should think I *would!* But how are you to get out of London? What excuse can you make to Mrs. Lascelles?"

She hated herself that she could lie to *him*, and yet such is the force of habit, such are the exigencies of a life like hers, the ready falsehood came glib to her tongue.

"We are all going to The Lilies for a day or two," she said. "Miss Hallaton is to be there, with Mrs. Lascelles, on a visit."

Even now he winced as if he was stung, at the bare mention of Helen's name. The sensation was painful in the extreme, though qualified by gratified vanity, and a certain bitter satisfaction in the justice of his reprisals.

She read him like a book. If she had ever

wavered for a moment, if her better nature had ever warned her to spare the man's future because she loved him, all such considerations were utterly set aside in that passion for rivalry which has driven so many women to destruction, and by which Miss Ross was certainly not less affected than the rest of her sex.

In all matters of love, war, pleasure, or business, Frank had a great idea of sailing with the tide. So long as things went smoothly, his maxim was to "let the ship steer herself," a method of navigation both safer and more successful than people generally imagine. He assented with the utmost devotion to all Jin's arrangements, even in their most trifling details, and did not even protest against her cruelty in cutting short their interview, and imperatively forbidding him to accompany her any part of the way home.

"You see I trust you in everything," said he, as he bade her "good-bye" at the door of the cab to which he consigned her.

"And do not I trust *you?*" was her answer,

with a look that spoke volumes, rousing all the manly impulses of his nature, appealing to all the generous instincts of his heart.

She knew exactly how to manage him. As she drove away, Frank felt that to deceive this simple, confiding girl, who had placed herself so completely at his mercy, trusted so implicitly in his honour, would be, of all villanies, the blackest and most disgraceful. "If I'm going to make a fool of myself," he muttered, while the rattle of her cab was lost in the roar of an adjacent thoroughfare, "at least you shall never find out I think so; and, come what may, my darling, hang me if I'll ever be such a rogue as to make a fool of *you!*"

Miss Ross, returning to No. 40, experienced much the same feelings as a whist-player, who, with unexpectedly good cards, has yet made the most of them by science, skill, and studious attention to the game. Perhaps, also, she felt conscious of a certain fatigue and depression, such as generally succeeds brain-work accompanied by excitement. During her *tête-à-tête* dinner with Mrs. Lascelles she was more silent than usual, whereas the other lady was more talkative. It did not escape the latter, however, that Jin's manner had acquired a softness and a wistful kindness towards herself she had never observed before. Uncle Joseph, too, coming to spend the evening, boiling with indignation, thought his ladye-love tenderer, more womanly, more attractive, than ever. She had coaxed him into good-humour with his first cup of tea, and in less than ten minutes had him in perfect subjection once more. Whether it was compunction or remorse, or only the innate coquetry inseparable from the woman, I cannot explain, but a charm seemed to hang about Jin to-night irresistible as the spells of a sorceress. Uncle Joseph, though the least sensitive of subjects, was completely subdued.

He took an early opportunity, however, of asking his enchantress, not without irritation, why she had been out when he called? Her answer disarmed him completely.

"I waited till past five, and then the pain

got so much worse, I could bear it no longer."

His heart leaped and his face brightened. "You—you don't mean you couldn't endure the anxiety! Miss Ross!—Jin! How I wish I'd known! How I wish I'd seen you! What! You—you actually started to look for me?"

"Not so bad as that," she answered, with a smile. "I went out to get a tooth stopped."

CHAPTER XXII.

KIDNAPPING.

"First for Windsor?—Second to Slough? which is it to be? I wish these young women knew their own minds!" muttered an irritated railway official at Paddington, as Miss Ross, changing her directions with inconvenient suddenness, blocked the stream of passengers defiling past his window to take their tickets for the train. She reinstated herself, however, in his good opinion, by unusual alacrity in paying her money, ere she entered the ladies' waiting-room, from which, after a couple of minutes, she reappeared, completely disguised in figure, face, and bearing.

She had gone in, a shapely, upright, good-looking young woman, on whom masculine eyes could not but turn with unqualified approval. She came out, wearing a double veil, a pair of blue spectacles, and a respirator, bent crooked, with one leg shorter than the other. Thus metamorphosed, she limped to her second-class carriage under the very noses of two men, to have been discovered by whom would have entailed ruin, disgrace, and instantaneous explosion of her grand scheme.

Picard and Frank, setting the bye-laws of the company at defiance, by smoking on its platform, were making indiscreet remarks on the appearance of the different passengers hurrying to take their places in the same train. Little did they think, how the heart was beating, of that dowdy, dumpy figure they glanced at half in pity, half in scorn; nor how a thrill of triumph pervaded her from top to toe, while Miss Ross reflected, with what transparent devices these lords of the creation were to be duped, with what facility she could turn and twist two great stupid men round her dainty little finger. She did not so much mind Frank. Had he been alone, they might have journeyed amicably down together, but she dreaded recognition by his companion ; above all she dreaded that Picard might have the same object as herself, might be going out of town for the express purpose of visiting the child. Even in this case, however, she felt a proud confidence in her own powers of outwitting them all ; conscious, that like an Indian amongst the rapids, she could steer to an inch, undismayed by any danger, however imminent, that did not actually overwhelm her bark, taking a keen wild pleasure in the very destruction she invited only to elude. Sitting opposite a motherly woman, with a basket, who sucked peppermint as a sailor "turns his quid," she found herself almost wishing she had taken her place boldly in the next carriage, which a strong odour of tobacco-smoke bade her infer was occupied by two men, both of whom she had successively fancied she loved.

Their conversation would have interested her no doubt. Having taken a great liking to Frank, ever since the opportune appearance of that champion on the night he was assailed, Picard had confided to him the whole history of a certain attraction that drew him so often to Windsor, and was now deep in a dissertation on the trustworthiness of Mrs. Mole, and the endearing qualities of her charge.

"Such a little brick, Captain," said the Confederate officer, between the puffs of an enormous cigar. "Such quality, such gumption, such grit, I wouldn't have believed could be found in a child, not if you raised 'em by steam! To see the critter's face when he lifts the latch, to let me in—he can just reach it, and very proud he is to be so tall. To hear him crow, and halloo, and sing 'Hail, Columbia!' 'God save the Queen,' 'Rule Britannia,' and 'Yankee Doodle.' He's got 'em all as ready as sharp-shooting, and as correct —as correct, as a barrel organ! It's my belief that child is destined to be a great man, Captain. He's gifted with adaptability, sir, and is what we call *capable.* That old woman I've trusted with him seems honest as the day, and does her duty by the varment *well.* Health, of course, at present, is the first consideration; but *you* see, when he gets a little older, if I don't give that boy an education, to fit him for any profession or position on earth—from stoker on this broad gauge railway to President of the United States! that's what I call bringing up a child in the way it should go."

Frank tried to appear more interested than he really felt.

"Exactly," said he; "and so whichever way he goes afterwards, must be the right one. It's an excellent plan, no doubt; but, I confess, I shouldn't have thought of it myself."

"They understand the question of education better on the other side of the Atlantic," continued Picard, in perfect good faith; "they go ahead there to some purpose in most things, but when they're working 'social science,' as they call it, the way they get the steam up is a caution! Well, I've concluded to take my own plan with the young one—I feel I've a right, for I couldn't love the boy better if he was my son ten times over. Ah! I sometimes think, Captain, I should have been a happier man if I had been a better one. Loafing is like smuggling, it don't pay in the long run. A contraband cargo is an awful risk, and a very uncertain profit; and yet, I doubt if it's a good thing, either, for a man to marry too early in life."

"Premature, eh?" answered Frank, not much encouraged, while conscious of feeling unpleasantly nervous, as he approached alike the termination of his journey and his bachelorhood. "Of course—certainly—thanks—yes, I will have another cigar—it brings him up short, I take it—settles him, as you may say, once for all."

Picard laughed. "Women *un*settle a chap sometimes," said he, "and bring him up short enough too, for that matter. I've tried it every way, and I only know I've always been wrong; but I sometimes think I could do better if I'd another chance. That's an uncommon likely girl now, that Miss Hallaton, as they call her. I wonder if I could do any good in those diggings. You know the family well, Captain; what do you think?"

Frank could hardly conceal his annoyance, though it was sad to reflect that after all he had no right to be angry. Loyal enough still to revere the flag he had deserted, he answered somewhat stiffly.

"Sir Henry looks very high for his daughter, and I should think Miss Hallaton herself would be more fastidious, more difficult to please, than most people."

Picard seemed in no way disconcerted. A life of adventure soon produces a habit of underrating difficulties, and a tendency to risk all for the chance of winning a part. I am not sure but that a spice of this kind of recklessness is appreciated by women, and that "nothing venture, nothing have," is a maxim which holds good in love, quite as much as in other affairs of life.

"Oh! I could get on well enough with the old man," said he; "there's a freemasonry amongst fellows of his stamp and mine. I consider Sir Henry quite one of my own sort, and, indeed, I've sounded him. Well, perhaps I can hardly say *sounded* him, on the subject, but hinted to him that he and I might do a smartish stroke of business if we put our money and our brains together, and played a little into each other's hands. It's the girl that beats *me*, Captain; that's where I'm at sea. She's got a high-handed way with her that I can't make head against at all, and I'm not easily dashed, far from it. The young woman's uneasy in herself, too. There's something on her mind. I saw it from the first. The best thing she can do, in my opinion, would be to marry some smart, likely young chap, who would take her abroad for a spell till her colour came back, and the nonsense was driven out of her head. I should like to be *him* uncommon! But I don't see my way."

There was much of bitter to Frank in this simple, confidential talk, dashed, nevertheless, with a something of sweet and subtle poison, that ought to have warned him he had no right to pledge himself to one woman while he could thus be affected by the mere name of another. Strange to say, he felt that Picard now constituted a link between himself and that past life which after to-day must be put out of sight for ever, and he clung to the Confederate officer accordingly.

"You'll come to luncheon at the barracks, of course," said he, throwing the end of his cigar out at the window. "I must be there till five or six o'clock to parade my young horses for the Colonel. Why he wants to see them to-day I don't know, considering he bought them all himself, and a very moderate lot they are. But, anyhow, *there* I shall be till five at the earliest."

"Luncheon," repeated Picard reflectively; "I don't care if I do. I'm generally peckish about two o'clock, and Britishers *do* dine unnaturally late. I'll go and see the boy first, come back to feed with you, and take a look at the young horses afterwards. How long now, Captain, do you estimate that it takes to get a trooper fit for duty?"

"How long?" repeated the other, who could be eloquent on this congenial theme. "Why, two years at the very least. And even then half of them are not properly mouthed for common field movements, certainly not for parade. Why,

I've seen a squadron of Austrian cuirassiers march off at a walk, every horse beginning like a foot soldier with his near leg, and I don't know why our cavalry should be worse drilled than theirs. One of my troop was actually run away with last year at a review, and I felt as much ashamed as if he had run away in action! No; what I want is to see more rides and fewer foot-parades, the men less bothered and the horses better broke."

"Well, you *do* take an unconscionable time over everything in this old, slow, and sure country," answered Picard. "Why, if we'd wanted two years, or two months either, to get our cattle fit for service, none of Stuart's best things would have come off at all. In ten days, Captain, ten days at most, I'd every horse in my squadron as steady as a time-piece, and as handy as a cotton-picker. I wish I could have shown you 'Stonewall.' I called him 'Stonewall' after Jackson, you may be sure. A great, slapping chestnut, sixteen hands high, and up to carrying two hundred pounds weight. Before I'd ridden him a week he'd lift a glove like a retriever, and walk on his hind legs like a poodle. I could tell you things of that horse that I'll defy *you*, or any man, to believe! I was riding him on the twenty-first of—— Halloo! here we are at Slough. What a queer old woman, hobbling along the platform! Now, that's the sort of figure you wouldn't see from one end of the States to the other. Where do you suppose they raised her, and what do you think she is?"

"Somebody's aunt, I should say," answered Frank carelessly, hardly vouchsafing a glance, as the train moved on; and Miss Ross drew a long breath of relief to find herself safe and undiscovered at Slough Station, within a few miles of her boy.

She thought well, however, to retain her disguise for the present, feeling such confidence in its efficiency that she regretted the first impulse of panic when she saw Picard should have prompted her to alter her destination. She reflected that, had she gone on to Windsor, she could have made sure of his proceedings, while remaining herself unrecognised, and that it would have been simpler and less trouble to watch the hawk than the nest. She must hover round the latter now, and so baffle this bird of prey, even in the very neighbourhood of its quarry.

So Miss Ross, putting more deformity into her figure, more limp into her gait, shrouding herself more sedulously in her veils, her spectacles, and her respirator, seized on a job-carriage she found unoccupied, and ordered its driver to proceed leisurely in the direction of The Lilies. She was glad to have half-an-hour's quiet, in which to think over her plans, undisturbed by the jingling of this unassuming conveyance, and felt her courage rising, her wits growing brighter, as the moments drew near to test the steadiness of the one and the quickness of the other.

It was a part of Jin's character, on which she prided herself not a little, that come what might she was always "equal to the occasion." As Picard said of her long ago, soon after that form of marriage which the woman believed to have been an imposition, and the man considered no more binding than any other contract it suited his convenience to dissolve, "she could dive deeper, and come up drier" than most people. Notwithstanding the desperate nature of the plunge she was now contemplating, Jin had no misgivings but that she would re-appear on the surface with plumage unruffled and confidence unimpaired.

Dismissing her fly at the gate of The Lilies, thereby leaving its driver to suppose that she was an upper servant belonging to that establishment, she took the well-remembered path leading to Mrs. Mole's cottage, limping along at a very fair pace over the open meadows, but availing herself of every leafy copse and thick luxuriant hedge that might hide her from the eyes of chance observers. No Indian "brave," on the war-path, could have been more cunning, more vigilant, more chary of leaving evidence where "the trail" had passed. At an angle of the road, within sight of the casket that held her jewel, an opportune hiding-place was formed by the intersection of two large strong fences, now tangled and impervious in a wealth of foliage, briars, and wild flowers. Here, in a nook concealing her from any passenger who did not pass directly in her front, Miss Ross disposed herself to wait and watch. A Berkshire farmer, slouching by in a tumble-down gig, was the only person who disturbed her solitude; and coming under his stolid gaze, she had presence of mind to pull a letter from her pocket and pretend to make a sketch. Watching his figure jogging drowsily down the road she shrank back in her hiding-place, for Picard was lifting the latch of Mrs. Mole's garden gate, and a little voice, in shrill accents that made her pulses leap, was bidding him welcome to the cottage. Jin's whole faculties seemed to concentrate themselves in her large wild shining eyes.

Would he never go? Did he mean to stay there all day? She looked at her watch again and again, while every quarter of an hour seemed lengthened to a week. With hungry jealousy she pictured him in the brick-floored kitchen, lifting her curly-haired darling on his knee, robbing her of the kiss, the smile, the simple prattle, the little endearments. She experienced a fierce desire to rush in and rescue her child by force. "What right has he to come between me and my boy?" thought she, clenching her hands with impatience. "I can understand what they mean now when they talk of the love a tigress bears for her cubs. Ah! *I* shouldn't have got tired of you so soon, my little pet," she added, with characteristic inconsistency, when the click of the front-door latch announced Picard's departure, and she saw him waving back a succession of "farewells" to the child.

He had remained with it really less than an hour. To Miss Ross the time seemed interminable, yet now it was over, she blamed him that his visit had been so short.

She forced herself to wait till he had been gone full ten minutes by her watch. Then, abandoning disguise, she scudded down the road, and, with a hasty greeting to Mrs. Mole, caught Gustave in her arms and strained him to her breast, as if she feared he would be torn away from her on the spot. The little fellow seemed quite pleased to see her again, laying his curly head to her cheek, and crowing out those inarticulate murmurs of fondness which are so touching from the innocent affection of a child. Jin's eyes filled with tears, but she had to hide them from Mrs. Mole, who, congratulating herself on such good fortune as two opportunities for gossip in one day, was careful not to let the occasion pass away unimproved.

"He's growed, miss, ain't he now?" asked that good woman, in a tone pleasantly contrasting with the stiffness of her demeanour on Jin's first appearance at the cottage. "An' he's a-learnin' to be a good boy, as well as a big boy, ain't ye, Johnnie? Why, the gentleman said as he hardly knowed him again, if it wasn't for his curls. Strange enough, miss, the gentleman hadn't but just only left as you come in. An' Johnnie he was wondering this morning, in his little bed, when the dark lady was a-coming to see him again, and if she'd bring him a plaything. Ah! miss, there's greater sense in childer' than in grown-up folks—isn't there now? An' greater gratitude too—the more you make of 'em, the better they like you, but it's not so with men and women."

Abstaining from discussion on the question thus opened up, Miss Ross produced the toy she had bought the day before, and it is hard to say whether the women, old and young, or the child itself, seemed most delighted by the shouts of triumph with which this acquisition was greeted. Gustave, or Johnnie, as Mrs. Mole called him, shook it, rung its bells, undressed it, and dressed it up again, idealizing it in turn as a soldier, a clergyman, a butter-churn, and, till checked by his careful guardian, a hearth-broom, with unbounded satisfaction, renewed at each fresh metamorphosis. And so the afternoon wore away till it was time for Miss Ross to prefer a long-considered petition, that she might take the child out for a walk.

But here a difficulty presented itself: Johnnie had a slight cold; the evening was clouding over, and threatened rain. It was only after long and earnest pleading that Mrs. Mole gave her consent for "one little turn" as far as the river and back, while she busied herself about some household matters that were more easily set to rights in the absence of her charge.

With a beating heart, Miss Ross led him down the pathway towards the river, the boy kicking out his feet and taking huge steps with his short legs in a state of high triumph and glee.

Presently, at the water's edge, he looked wistfully up in his companion's face and asked—

"Ain't we going back? Never going back—never—no more?"

"Would you *like* never to go back, darling?" said Jin, stooping to fold him in her arms.

"I want to go back to Moley!" answered Johnnie, now panic-stricken, and making up his face for a cry.

Heavy drops of rain began to fall, and at the same moment a boat, shooting suddenly round a bend in the river, grated its keel on the shallows under the bank.

CHAPTER XXIII.

"STRANGERS YET."

The rower of this boat, whose back was necessarily turned to the shore, wore a pea-jacket, with its collar turned up to the brim of a black hat, such as is not usually affected by watermen, either professional or amateur. Through Jin's beating heart shot a sickening throb of misgiving and alarm. She turned cold and faint, catching up her boy and hugging him instinctively to her breast.

As the rower, obviously unused to an oarsman's exercise, rose, straightened himself, and turned round, he started with a violence that shot the boat back into deep water, her chain running out with a clang over her bows. Stupefied as it seemed by this apparition of the man whom she had watched from Mrs. Mole's door three hours ago, Jin's eyes dilated, her jaw dropped, while she gazed in Picard's face as if she had been turned to stone.

He was the first to recover himself, and burst into a laugh, not entirely forced.

"Who would ever have thought it?" said he, shoving the boat close in shore. "Of all reunions this is the most extraordinary, the most unlooked for. Jump in, Madame, there is no time to lose: in ten minutes it will rain like a water-spout. Great heavens, you are unaltered after all these years, and you have not a grey hair in your head!"

She obeyed mechanically in silence, folding Gustave beneath her shawl, who protested with energy against the embarkation, expressing a strong desire to return to "Old Moley" forthwith.

Once more in mid-stream, Picard laid on his oars as if doubtful whether to proceed. "What are you doing with that boy?" he asked.

She had recovered her presence of mind,

though still confused and bewildered, as after some stunning blow.

"You *know* me, Achille," said she, bending on him the defiant, impracticable gaze he remembered so well. "Whatever happens, wherever we are bound, the child goes with me! Where are you taking us? What is the meaning of it all?"

Picard's face was not improved by the diabolical expression that swept over it. "The meaning is this," he answered in a hoarse whisper: "I am helping Captain Vanguard to run away with my own—bah!" he broke off abruptly, "there will be time enough for explanations between here and Windsor bridge: the question is now about the child. He must not go a yard farther—he'll be wet to the skin as it is. There are few things I wouldn't part with to—to—undo the wrongs between you and me; but I cannot, and will not, give up the boy!"

She would have been fiercer in all probability, but that Picard, accepting the heavy down-pour, which now commenced, in his thin summer waistcoat and shirt-sleeves, had stripped off his pea-coat, and was wrapping the boy carefully in its folds, without however removing him from his mother's embrace. The little fellow smiled, and tugged playfully at this rugged nurse's whiskers, obviously welcoming the face of a friend, but repeated his request to return to "Old Moley" as speedily as possible.

"I mean to have no discussions," said Jin, in tight, concentrated accents that denoted suppressed rage and inflexible resolution. "I never wished to see your face again, and I shall insist presently on knowing why you are here now; but in the meantime I desire to know what right you have to the child."

"I like that!" exclaimed Picard with a bitter laugh. "Rather, what right have you? I saved his life!"

"I gave him birth!" answered Jin collectedly. "This is the infant you deserted so gallantly and so generously when you left his mother. Enough! He has no claim on you, my precious; you belong solely and exclusively to *me!*"

Picard heeded not. Bending over that little bundle, folded so carefully in his pea-jacket, on its mother's knee, he kissed the soft brow tenderly, gently, almost reverently, while a tear hanging in the man's shaggy whiskers, dropped on the pure delicate cheek of the child.

"No wonder I loved you," he muttered. "I wish I had been a better man, for your sake."

Miss Ross was touched. "*Allons!*" said she; "you and I may come to an understanding, after all. Speak the truth and so will I. How did you find the boy, and where?"

Ashamed of his feelings, as such men usually are ashamed of any one redeeming point in a character saturated with evil, he had recovered his emotion, and was pulling leisurely down stream with the utmost composure.

"How and where?" he repeated. "Well, the story is simple enough, and there would be nothing extraordinary in it, but for what I have this moment learned, I give you my honour, for the first time. I happened to be at Lyons in one of the worst floods they had there for twenty years. The river rose incredibly during the night, and I was out at daybreak to—to see the fun, you know, and render any assistance I could afford. In the top room of a cottage, completely undermined and tottering, I saw a woman making signals of distress. Between us lay what looked like a canal: it may have been a street once for all I know, but a few defaced walls, five or six feet above the water-level, were alone left. Excepting the half-fallen cottage from which this woman waved her arms, not a tenement was standing for some score of yards on each side. I was already immersed to my waist, but I had to swim for it before I could reach the poor creature, who seemed out of her wits with terror. Treading water a few feet below, I implored her to plunge in at once, and trust to me. I thought she was coming, when '*Tiens!*' she screamed out—I can hear her now—and threw, as I imagined, a linen bundle at my head. It fell beyond me, and sank immediately. I dived for it, and quickly too; but while I was under water the walls fell with a crash, and the whirl carried me several paces from where I had gone down, not, however, before I had succeeded in grasping the bundle, which I brought with me to the surface. As the rush subsided I found the stream encumbered with dust, beams, household furniture, but of the woman I could see nothing. Doubtless at the instant, perhaps from the very effort she made to consign me her burthen, its foundations gave way, and she fell among the ruins of her house, to be drowned without a chance of escape.

"The bundle contained a boy—living, unhurt, and very wet. I have taken care of him ever since. There he is. Do you think anything would tempt me to part from him now?"

The tears rose to Jin's eyes. "God bless you!" said she. "You saved my child!"

"I saved *our* child," he answered; "and I am not going to give him up."

"Why are you here to-day?" she asked. "And where do you mean to put me ashore?"

She was meditating, even then, how she might escape him; if to reach Frank Vanguard, well and good; but, at any rate, to attain some refuge where she could be alone with her child.

He laughed, to cover a strong sense of embarrassment, even of shame.

"This is a strange *rencontre*," he said. "It must be Fate. You and I have never once met among all the amusements of a London season; and we meet now in the rain, on the lonely river, at a time when we ought most to forget and ignore each other's existence. Of all people in the world, I must be the last you would have wished to come across to-night."

"En effet," she muttered, "c'est un rencontre assez mal-à-propos."

Her coolness seemed contagious. He proceeded with a *sang-froid* too complete to be perfectly natural:—

"I came here to oblige my dearest friend, a man for whom I would make almost any sacrifice. That foreign prince at Windsor has taken a sudden fancy to inspect a regiment of Household Cavalry in their barracks. He is there at this moment, attended by every officer available for duty. My friend Captain Vanguard came to me in the greatest agitation. He had a rendezvous, he said, for this evening with a lady. It could not be put off. It was of the gravest importance. If he failed to appear, she was lost. He reposed entire confidence in my honour. He asked my advice. What was to be done? I considered. I remembered my obligations to him. I put myself in his place. In short, here I am, *in* his place, pledged to conduct you safely to the Castle Hotel, there to wait till he is at leisure to join you, after which I am free to take whatever course I think due to my own character in this most awkward complication. I need not say that it never entered my head the Miss Ross I had heard of in society, or the lady whose *enlèvement* I was to conduct for my friend, could be—well—could be *you!* Madame, we have met in a manner that is creditable to neither of us—that is utterly ruinous to one. Can we not ignore this clumsy *contretemps?* Can we not agree to conceal it, and never meet again?"

Jin felt much reassured by this climax, though

ready to sink with shame and vexation at the whole business.

"You know I am going to—to *marry* Captain Vanguard," she said, looking him straight in the face, though she hesitated a little in her sentence. "Will you promise to throw no impediment in my way—to keep your own counsel? In short, to let bygones be bygones, if, on my part, I consent to leave the past unscrutinized and unavenged?"

"It's a fair offer," he replied; "but I cannot give you up the boy."

"Then war to the knife!" she burst out recklessly. "I will lose husband, lover, home, character, everything—life itself—rather than part with Gustave for a day!"

Perhaps he knew what a desperate woman was. Perhaps—for, in his own way, he too loved little Gustave very dearly—he reflected that a child might safely be committed to a mother's tenderness, even were that mother the wildest and most wilful of her sex. In a couple of minutes his busy brain formed a thousand schemes, took in a thousand contingencies. Frank Vanguard was about to marry the woman who had once held a wife's place at his hearth. Well, to that he had no objection. He would at least be freed from an awkward claim, which might interfere with certain vague schemes of his own that had only recently begun to take a shape. In those schemes Frank's assistance, as a friend of Sir Henry Hallaton's, might be valuable. An intimacy with Vanguard, and the latter's good word, would vouch at least for his position and standing in society. Helen could no longer consider him a mere unknown adventurer. Some influence he might obtain over Frank through his wife, if, indeed, this wild, untoward marriage were to come off. His chief difficulty lay in that wife's inflexible and impracticable character; but surely he could bend her to his will through her affection for the boy.

"You cannot take him with you now," observed Picard, in a perfectly matter-of-fact tone. "Think of the travelling, and the weather, and the ridicule attached to the whole proceeding. You are not going to join your future husband, surely, with a ready-made child?"

"I *am!*" she exclaimed, in high indignation. "Frank knows all about it, and takes us as we are!"

"Then I may explain everything," said he, pulling on faster, as if satisfied. "It makes it much easier for me as regards my duty to my friend."

She saw her false position, and felt she was now at his mercy.

"Let us make a bargain," she said. "I would not injure *you;* I hope you would not injure *me.* I confess I have deceived Captain Vanguard in this matter. I told him about Gustave, but I said he was a sister's son. I cannot part with the child. I implore you to let me keep him! If you will consent so far, and abstain from crossing my path at this the turning-point of my whole life's happiness, I will swear to absolve you, formally and in writing, from any claim I may have on your property or your personal freedom; and if ever I can be of service to you, or advance your career in any way, so help me heaven, I will!"

Picard pondered. She had made the very proposal he would himself have broached; but he was too crafty to betray satisfaction, and, to do him justice, felt very loath to lose the child none the less that he had now discovered it was his own. Yet he could not but reflect that so long as Gustave remained with her by his consent, he had the mother at a disadvantage, and could drive her which way he would. Frank Vanguard's domestic happiness would thus be at his mercy, and it was strange if, with consummate knowledge of the world, and utter freedom from scruples, he could not turn such a power to good account.

"Agreed," said he, as they shot past the Brocas clump, and caught sight of Windsor Castle, looming gigantic through a leaden atmosphere of mist and rain. "Agreed. We are strangers again from henceforth as regards Vanguard—as regards the world. When we meet in society, that is to be clearly understood. But we are *not* strangers as regards our boy. Once a week you will write and tell me of his welfare. Once a month you will arrange that I shall see him, either with or without witnesses—I care not which. Stay! I have it. You shall tell Vanguard I am the father of your dead sister's child! Capital! I begin to think I have quite a genius for intrigue!"

"It is such a tissue of falsehood!" she groaned; "and Frank is so honest—so trustful!"

He ground his teeth; but forced himself to answer with unwavering accents and a smooth brow.

"I cannot enter into the sentiment of the thing. You know me of old. That is my ultimatum. Take it or leave it. I must run you ashore here, and I can show you the short cut to the hotel."

"Agreed!" she whispered, as he handed her along a quivering plank that let her reach the shore dry-shod. "Honour?"

"Even among thieves," he added, with a

laugh; and thus was the contract ratified on both sides.

But short as was that by-way from the river to the Castle Hotel, heavily as the rain came down, enforcing the utmost attention to little Gustave—a perishable article indeed "to be kept dry, this side uppermost"—and fractious as was the deportment of that inexperienced traveller who, thoroughly bewildered with his situation, retained but the one idea of bewailing his lot aloud, while he held on manfully to the new toy, Jin found time to arrive at the noblest, the grandest, and the most important resolution she had ever made in her life.

It has always appeared to me there is one infallible criterion of that rare and mysterious affection which goes by the name of true love. "How many *dollars* do you like her?" asked a Yankee of the friend who expatiated on his devotion to a beloved object; thus gauging, as he considered, that devotion by a standard at once unerring, and not to be misconceived. The friend, "estimating" that he "liked her a thousand dollars," proved himself ten times more to be depended on than his rival, who only "liked her a hundred;" and, in my opinion, there was much knowledge of human nature in this Yankee's mode of valuing an attachment. If you own but five dollars in the world, and you "love your love five-dollars' worth," you are very much in love with her indeed, and have come triumphantly through that strongest test of sincerity which consists in self-sacrifice.

There must have been a spark of sacred fire under the lurid flame which Frank had kindled in her breast, or Miss Ross would have escaped a struggle that seemed to tear her heart in pieces during this short wet walk with all its accompanying annoyances—that made her unconscious of heavy rain, draggled garments, and unwelcome company—that, but for a mother's instinct, would have caused her to forget the necessity of sheltering her boy.

She stole a glance—it was well he did not observe it—at the hated form of the man by her side, and all the masculine part of her nature rebelled in the remembrance of its former thraldom. The thought of Frank Vanguard's open brow, of his loving eyes, his manly, kindly smile, and feminine instincts of tender generosity, rose strong within her as she turned scornfully from the suggestion that he, her own, who had chosen her so nobly, so chivalrously, should be at the mercy of such a man as Picard. "No!" thought Jin, walking on very fast, and hugging Gustave tighter than ever to her breast. "Better that I should never see him again, than fasten such a clog round his neck! Better that I should lose my one dear chance on earth, than ruin him, degrade him, drag him down to the level of such people as ourselves! I am not to be happy, it seems, in that way; but I have no right to complain since I have got my child. And yet, Frank, Frank, what will you think of me? You will never know the sacrifice I made for you! You will never know what it cost me! You will never know that I loved you better than my very life!"

While such thoughts were racking heart and

brain, it was quite in accordance with Jin's character that her outward manner should be more than ordinarily composed and self-possessed. Arriving at the welcome shelter of the Castle Hotel, she desired a fire to be kindled immediately, and taking very little notice of Picard, busied herself with the child and its wet things. He was quiet enough now; but moaned at intervals as if uneasy in mind rather than in body; but it did not escape a mother's observation that the cheek he pressed against her own was hotter than usual, and though it made his dark eyes shine so beautifully, she would rather not have seen that brilliant colour so deep and strong. But it was a time for action, not for apprehension, and she turned to Picard with a quiet gesture of authority, such as she would have used towards a servant—

"Be so good as ring the bell," she said, "and tell them to get some bread and milk for this little boy. Order tea in an hour, and then go to the barracks and tell Captain Vanguard I am waiting here. I suppose I shall not see you again—good-bye."

He took the hand she held out, with something of admiration and respect.

"Well, you *are* a cool one!" he exclaimed. "I declare, you're cooler even than *me!* In a matter like this, where there's interest in one scale and feeling in the other, I think I can trust you as I would myself!"

She only nodded, resuming the occupation, from which she had turned for a moment, of drying her child's wet socks at the lately-kindled fire. Picard caught the boy in his arms and smothered him with kisses; then replacing him in his mother's lap, took his departure without another word.

"Where's he going?" said Gustave, making a plunge, to land barefooted on the floor.

"He's going away, dear," answered Jin, much pre-occupied, and scorching the socks against the bars of the grate. "And we're going away too. Don't you want to go away from this nasty room?"

"I want to go to Moley," answered the boy, in a sing-song that frequent repetition on the river had rendered mechanical. "And I want my tupper," he added, brightening up at so happy an afterthought.

But he couldn't eat his supper when it came; and now that his things were dry, Miss Ross was glad to hush him off to rest in her arms.

When he was sound asleep she rang the bell gently. "I am going out for an hour," said she to the waiter. "If anybody calls, say that tea is ordered to be ready when I come back."

Then she walked away in the pouring rain, and beckoned a flyman from the stand.

"Drive to The Lilies," she said in a loud voice. "Shut those glasses, and make haste."

But as soon as they were clear of the town she reversed her sailing orders, and directed the man to proceed to Staines.

Arriving at the station, she found by a time-table that an up-train was due in five minutes. "What do you charge for waiting?" asked Miss Ross, as the driver let her out.

The man informed and overcharged her.

"Then wait here for the down-train in an hour," said she, paying him liberally. "If you don't get a fare you can then drive back to Windsor; but I shall desire the station-master to see that you remain here on the chance."

So, hushing Gustave, who, considering he seemed so sleepy, was strangely restless, Miss Ross took her place in the train, to be whirled to town with the comfortable reflection that, till her fly returned to Windsor, in two hours time, it would be impossible for Frank Vanguard to obtain any trace of her, while she herself would be in the labyrinth of London in forty minutes. She pulled the double veil from her pocket, and dropped it over her face, while she rocked the boy tenderly on her knee.

It was well for him to have this protection, for Gustave did not need another wetting, and his mother was crying as if her heart would break.

Thus it fell out that Frank, flying on the wings of love and a thorough-bred hack from his duty at the barracks to his affianced at the Castle

Hotel, found nothing there but a black fire, an empty room, and a waiter's assurance that "the lady would be back in less than half-an-hour. She'd been gone longer nor that already."

Picard, of course, having fulfilled his mission, considered himself absolved from further attendance, and Frank had nothing more to do but walk up and down the cheerless apartment, fussing, fuming, wondering, and, I fear, at times unable to restrain an oath. The rain fell, the evening waned, the twilight turned to dark, and at length the waiter came in with candles, and asked "if he should bring in tea?"

Then Frank could stand it no longer, but rushed wildly out to make inquiries, invoking a hideous and totally undeserved fate on the waiter and the tea.

CHAPTER XXIV.

GREENWICH.

But Captain Vanguard was not the only person whom the inexplicable disappearance of Miss Ross overwhelmed with consternation and dismay. Picard, whom, of course, he consulted first, affected to treat the matter lightly, vowing there must have been some misconception of directions, some misunderstanding about the time, while in his heart he cursed the invincible wilfulness, the inflexible obstinacy that, he knew of old, would dare and endure anything rather than give way. He did his best, we may be sure, to help his friend, in hunting down the woman who had outwitted him; but the track of a fugitive is soon lost in London, and, with all his craft, Picard's best was done in vain. For Vanguard, he considered this disappointment the luckest thing that could happen. For his own part, he never wanted to see Miss Ross again; but it was a sharp, keen pang, to think that every tie must now be cut off between himself and his boy. Even Jin would have pitied him, had she known how he suffered under this privation.

Poor old Mrs. Mole, too, nearly went distracted with alarm, anxiety, and remorse. After running in and out of her cottage all the evening, till, to use her own expression, "she hadn't a dry thread anywheres, an' the damp had fixed itself in her bones," she started off at dark to take counsel of the parish clerk, the turnpike-man, and a neighbouring cow-doctor; from none of whom, as may be supposed, did she gather much counsel or comfort. The clerk was "sure as the lad would be back afore mornin';" the turnpike-man opined "he'd runned away for aggravation; and if 'twas his'n, *he'd* soon let him know not to try *them* games no more;" while the cow-doctor, not exactly sober, opined "he'd fell in o' the water, and drownded hisself, poor thing! and now the little varmint's gone to heaven, mayhap, and don't want to come back here no more."

The poor old woman, returning home from this futile expedition, to see Johnnie's little bed spread out, smooth and untumbled, as if waiting for the child, burst into a fit of crying, and sat all night through by the waning fire, with her apron thrown over her head.

On Uncle Joseph's feelings, when, calling at No. 40, he learned that Miss Ross had left her home without stating where she was going, or when she would return, I cannot take upon me to expatiate. Displeasure, perhaps, was the strongest sensation that affected him, but a fit of the gout arriving at this juncture to divert his attention from mental worry to bodily pain, he got through the ordeal altogether better than might have been expected.

Mrs. Lascelles, however, grew seriously alarmed and distressed, when the lapse of a second day brought no tidings of her inseparable companion and fast friend. She reproached herself bitterly for taking Jin to task about her conduct with Captain Vanguard. She contrasted her own comfortable home, all the luxuries that surrounded her, with a mental picture she chose to draw of Miss Ross, starving, in proud silence, on cold mutton, somewhere in a "second floor back," and felt painfully humiliated in the comparison. Then she wondered if it would be possible to track her by means of detectives, advertisements, "Pollaky's private inquiry office," or a heart-rending appeal in the agony column of the "Times." Finally, womanlike, feeling she must have somebody to lean on, she bethought her of Goldthred, and wrote him a pretty little note, marked "Immediate," desiring him to come and see her without delay. Why not Sir Henry? Mrs. Lascelles asked herself that question more than once; and, while searching her heart for the answer, made a discovery which by no means increased her respect for her own stability in sentiment or discrimination of character.

"Sir Henry would laugh," she thought, "and murmur some cynical remarks, half good-natured, half contemptuous, on women's friendships and women's fancies. He would help me, I have no doubt, and very likely, if he could find Miss Ross, might make love to her on his own account, but he would not take the matter up as if it was life and death to him, like Mr. Goldthred. I do declare, if I asked that man to get me a China rose, he'd go to China *for* it, rather than I should be disappointed. It must be very nice to believe in anybody as he believes in me. If I was only as good as he thinks I am! I wish I was! I wonder if I should be, supposing—supposing—— Well, the first thing is to find out poor dear Jin, and implore her to come back, if I have to go for her on my bare knees!"

So her letter was written and posted, Mrs. Lascelles never doubting that the recipient would answer it in person ere three hours had elapsed. But when the clock struck again and again, when luncheon passed without his appearance, and the summer afternoon waned, bringing no Mr. Goldthred, Mrs. Lascelles could not decide whether she felt most hurt, vexed, angry, disappointed, or distressed.

No doubt, if he had known such a letter was coming, he would have ignored other business without scruple, and remained at home to receive it all day; but Goldthred had left his own house for the City directly after breakfast, having no intention of returning to dress for dinner, because he had cut out for himself some fifteen hours' work that he must get through in less than twelve.

Of this task, the hardest part, in his estimation, was the entertainment of a large and rather *loud* party he had invited to dine with him at Greenwich. From these friends he felt there would be no escape till eleven o'clock at night.

It will be remembered that Goldthred, in an hour of exuberant feeling, had tried to organise a pic-nic, which unfortunately fell through from the inability to attend of those he was most anxious to invite. In such cases, however, some responsibility is almost always incurred by the adhesion of a few less important guests, who must nevertheless be provided with food and amusement, though the others are unable to come.

For Goldthred, indeed, there was no difficulty in substituting with these makeweights a Greenwich dinner-party for a Maidenhead pic-nic. Stray men were soon recruited to fill up the necessary complement. Failing ladies of higher calibre, Mrs. Battersea and Kate Cremorne were persuaded to enliven the gathering with their beauty, their dresses, and their mirth. Picard, who was glad of any scheme to take him away from Frank Vanguard, in that officer's present state of perturbation, agreed to drive them all down on his coach; and thus it fell out that Goldthred, with his heart rather sore about Mrs. Lascelles, little dreaming a letter from her was at that moment lying on his table, found himself sitting, in a glare of sunshine, by an open window, overlooking the river, between Mrs. Battersea and Kate Cremorne.

Two or three hot waiters were bringing in as many dishes, with imposing covers, that would have served for a burlesque feast in a pantomime.

Shawls, fans, hats, parasols, and overcoats, lay scattered about the room; men lounged and straddled in uncomfortable attitudes, as not knowing how to dispose of their limbs and persons; a confusion of many tongues prevailed; and above the babble rose Mrs. Battersea's voice, clear, shrill, and dominant, like the steam-whistle of a railway through the puffing diapason of the engine and continuous roar of the advancing train.

"I vote against waiting," dictated that imperious lady, when the probability was hazarded of a fresh batch of guests arriving later. "Never wait dinner for anybody, particularly at Greenwich. Now, Mr. Goldthred, don't be shy, take the top of the table. I'll sit by you here. Kate, support him on the other side. Sir Henry, come next me. I won't have you by Kate. I know what you're going to say—you'd rather be close to me, and have her to look at. I'm so tired of those old compliments. I wish men would find out something new! *Rangez vous, Messieurs! Le jeu est fait. Rien n'va plus!*"

"*Rouge gagne, et couleur,*" whispered Sir Henry Hallaton, with a glance at Mrs. Battersea's brilliant complexion and toilette to match, accompanied by a jerk of his elbow in his next neighbour's ribs. The latter, who had never been to Baden or Homburg, and whose French was that of "Stratford-atte-Bow," did not the least understand, so laughed heartily, and Sir Henry set him down in his own mind as "a pleasant young fellow, with a great idea of fun." The baronet had turned up at this gathering, as he generally did turn up wherever gaiety and absence of restraint were likely to prevail. Notwithstanding his better reason and his good resolutions, he was fast drifting down the stream of easy self-indulgence, which sooner or later carries a man so helplessly out to sea.

He had now struck up a close alliance with Picard, whereby that scheming adventurer hoped he might win his way into Helen's good graces, and so attain a certain standing-point in society, from which to push his fortunes with a daring energy that ought to command success. Sir

Henry could not, or would not, see the false position in which he placed himself by affecting such terms of intimacy with such a man.

The dinner was good enough, and to Goldthred seemed almost interminable, although exerting himself to do his duty towards his guests; he reaped a reward by gradually sliding into amusement in their conversation, and before the devilled white-bait came on, began even to interest himself in their society. The latter sentiment was due to the good feeling of Miss Cremorne, who, guessing her host was somewhat overweighted by his company, and altogether depressed in spirits, exerted herself very successfully to cheer him up, and bring him, as she expressed it, "out of the downs."

Kate did not miscalculate her own powers; indeed few men could have long resisted her low pleasant tones, kindly glances, and soft, sympathising manner; for notwithstanding high spirits, high courage, high temper, and sometimes high words, she could be gentle on occasion, and when Kate *was* gentle, she became simply irresistible.

Neglecting a dandy on her right, who accepted that calamity with the utmost philosophy, she devoted herself to Goldthred, till they grew so confidential, that when dinner was over, he brought his coffee-cup and cigar to a little corner she had purposely reserved by her side on the balcony. She was so unused to shyness amongst men, there was something so different from all her previous experience of his sex in Goldthred's simple, honest nature, homely though courteous manner, and utter absence of pretension, that she positively felt interested in him, and Miss Cremorne was the last young person in the world to be ashamed of the sentiment, or afraid to exhibit it.

"Why don't you offer me a cigar?" said she, with a killing glance that would have finished any other man in the room on the spot.

"You shall have a dozen," he answered, pulling out a well-filled case in some confusion. "I really didn't know you smoked."

"No more I do," she replied, laughing, "except sometimes a very tiny cigarette. No; I don't want one now; but that's no reason you shouldn't offer it. Don't you know, Mr. Goldthred, that with ladies you should always take the initiative?"

"It's so difficult," he answered doubtfully, sliding into the corner by her side. "One is never sure how far one ought to go, and I have the greatest horror of being a bore."

"There you're wrong," decided Kate;—"women *like* bores. For the matter of that, so does everybody. Who are the people that get on in society? Bores. Who manage your clubs, your race-meetings, your amusements? Bores. Who make the best marriages, keep the best houses, and insist on having all the pleasant people to dance attendance on them? Bores—bores—bores! They are in the majority, they have the upper hand, and they mean to keep it. Shall I tell you why? A bore is always in earnest; the more in earnest the greater bore! Have I made out my case?"

"At least you have given me a claim to bore *you*," said Goldthred, laughing.

"And *without* being in earnest," she replied; "though I think you could be very much in earnest with some people. That's why I'm interested in you. That's why I'm going to give you a piece of advice. There is an English proverb I need not repeat about 'a faint heart.' There is a French one more to the purpose, I think in your case, 'il faut se faire valoir.' Now, you mustn't flirt with me any longer. You'll hear of it again if you do, and two of my admirers are looking as black as thunder already. Go and circulate among your guests, but don't forget my advice, and good luck to you!"

Il faut se faire valoir. The words rang in his ears all the evening—through the bustle of breaking-up, the noisy departure, the chatter, and clatter, and hurry of the drive back to London—the very wheels seemed to tell it over and over in monotonous refrain, and ere Goldthred was set down at his own door, this sentence and its meaning seemed indelibly impressed on his brain.

Passing through the sitting-room, he found a

letter in the well-known handwriting, lying on his table, and although a thrill went through every nerve in his body, I think even then Kate's advice was beginning to bear fruit. On reading the epistle, no doubt, there came a re-action, and his first impulse was to rush at once to No. 40, notwithstanding the hour, the occasion, and the proprieties; his second, to write an answer then and there, expressing love, worship and devotion with an eloquence none the less burning from the convivialities of a Greenwich dinner-party; his third, and wisest, to let everything stand over till to-morrow. And then, while he assisted her to the best of his abilities, to teach his scornful lady, quietly but distinctly, that he had learnt by heart this new maxim—*Il faut se faire valoir!*

CHAPTER XXV.

HOW THEY MISSED HER.

So the London season drew towards its close, speeding merrily for some, dragging wearily for others, wearing on surely for all. It produced its usual crop of marriages, jiltings, slanders, and other embarrassments, but throughout the little circle of individuals, with whom we are concerned at present, the engrossing topic was still that mysterious disappearance of Miss Ross. No stone had been left unturned to find her out, and yet, so well did she take her measures, not a trace could be discovered. Two people, indeed, received tidings of the fugitive, but on each her letters impressed the hopelessness of a search, and the writer's determination to remain henceforth in complete seclusion. To Mrs. Mole, Miss

Ross sent a long and consolatory epistle, containing earnest assurance of the boy's safety, and an account of his sayings and doings, not forgetting many messages to "his old Moley," which would have gladdened her heart exceedingly but for the one drawback, that the little fellow lay ill with a feverish cold, and did not get stronger so fast as could be wished. To Frank Vanguard she wrote a few short lines, telling him she was not fit to be his wife—the only good deed she had ever done in her life, she said, was that which seemed to him the most cruel, the most perfidious; and all endeavours to hunt her out would not only be sheer waste of time, but also considered so many insults and injuries directed against herself. Though it did not entirely suspend his exertions, Frank's zeal was somewhat damped by this communication, which he lost no time in imparting to the circle of friends whom Jin had left overwhelmed with anxiety on her behalf. Uncle Joseph's gout, converging favourably to the extremities, gave him little time to think of anybody but himself. It took him to

Buxton, where the successive duties of drinking, driving, dressing, bathing, and dining at five o'clock, left not a moment of the day unoccupied, and where the constant contemplation of greater sufferers and more hopeless cripples afforded moral lessons every five minutes, tending to content and thankfulness that he was no worse.

Mrs. Lascelle's did, indeed, get hold of some idle tale about Uncle Joseph's attentions to a fascinating widow, also gouty, and of a brisk flirtation carried on by the enamoured couple, each in a Bath chair. Her informant stated, with what degree of truth I cannot take upon me to affirm, that this promising affair only exploded from the indiscretion of Mr. Groves, who, possessing himself of the lady's hand in the warmth of his protestations, unadvisedly seized the gouty one, and inflicted such pain, that she called out loudly before the whole Parade. But as this piece of tittle-tittle was related to his kinswoman by a lady, who heard it from another lady, who had seen it in the letter of a third, I submit it is not evidence, neither has it anything to do with the present history. On Mrs. Lascelles herself the disappearance of so firm a friend and confederate produced an effect that rendered her more than usually open to sympathy, and eager for consolation. She felt less confidence than heretofore in herself and her own resources. Solitude was bad enough, and doubly dispiriting after the society of so lively a companion, but the sense of having been deceived with her eyes open was worse than all. Occasional twinges of remorse, too, tormented her sadly, reminding her that she had spoken out so freely to one whom she ought to have been very careful of offending as dependent on herself. Of course, too, she put off her trip to Brighton, and her London engagement-book, originally compiled by Jin, naturally got into confusion, when deprived of that lady's supervision. Altogether Mrs. Lascelles felt keenly the want of somebody to lean on, and caught herself more than once thinking of her loneliness and her staunch admirer, Mr. Goldthred, with tears in her eyes!

Notwithstanding his confidence in Kate Cremorne's knowledge of the world, I doubt whether this gentleman would have possessed strength of mind to follow her advice had he been a free agent at the present crisis; but it so happened that some trustee-business, with which he was mixed up, required his personal supervision at the other end of England, and Goldthred, *nolens volens*, was forced to absent himself temporarily from her vicinity, who made all the sunshine, and, it must be confessed, most of the shade, in his harmless, uneventful life. Nothing could be more opportune than this enforced separation for furtherance of the object on which, no doubt, his whole heart was fixed. Judicious contrast seems in all art the secret of effect. Surprise, which has been called the essence of wit, is also the prime element of interest. Gentleness from a rough, firmness from an effeminate nature, constancy where we had reason to expect change, but, above all, self-assertion from the slave too long incarcerated and kept down, rouse us, as it were, to a sense of our own shortsightedness in matters that most affect our welfare, and warn us that in the affections as in other affairs of humanity, there is no solid foundation, no security, no repose. Then we begin to value this bird, whose wings are grown, and spread already for a flight. Let her but soar away to disappear in the dim horizon, and all the gold of Arabia seems inadequate to buy her back into the cage once more. Alas! that the lightest feather from her wing should be more precious now we have lost her than was the whole of that gentle, winsome creature when she made her nest in our bosom, and pecked the sugar from our lips, and perched daily in saucy security on her owner's loving hand. Could Goldthred, closeted with lawyers and perusing deeds in a murky manufacturing town, have appeared suddenly before the woman who was never five minutes out of his mind, and asked in waking reality the question he was always asking in his dreams, I think he might have made himself secure, once for all, from the rivalry even of Sir Henry Hallaton.

That easy-going gentleman, notwithstanding

his philosophy, his good humour, and the elastic nature of his conscience, was at present exceedingly pre-occupied and ill at ease. One may say that he had been dipped over head in the infernal river, as was Achilles; but like the son of Peleus, and every other hero I ever heard of, he retained his one vulnerable point, though it did not lie at his heel. To hit Sir Henry in a vital place it was necessary to aim at Helen. Alas! that the bow had not been drawn at random, nor had the arrow missed its mark!

She was composed as usual, and went about her daily occupations with the same calm manner, the same gentle methodical firmness as before, but to her father's loving eye there was something wanting, something amiss. As a practised musician detects the flat tones of an instrument not strung to concert-pitch, so the slightest discord jars on the senses of that true affection which renders all the perceptions painfully discerning and acute.

"You are not well, my child," said Sir Henry, one hot summer's morning soon after the mysterious disappearance of Miss Ross, which Helen connected instinctively with Captain Vanguard, though too proud to inquire how far that injudicious young officer was concerned in such a catastrophe. "You are not well, dear, and you hide it for fear of making your old father uncomfortable. You don't go out enough, or it's this cursed weather, or something. We must amuse you, my darling. You're getting hipped. I'm the same myself sometimes. Did you go to the Opera last night after all?"

"No, papa," was the answer; "I was too tired, and went to bed instead."

"Did you drive out yesterday? I met your aunt coming here to take you."

"No, papa—it was so hot."

"What are you going to do to-day?"

"Nothing, papa. I think—"

"Helen, Helen, this will never do," burst out Sir Henry, smoothing her hair with a caress habitual to him from her childhood, a caress that brought the tears into her large soft eyes. "You're moped, you're miserable, and I feel as if it was my fault for being papa instead of mamma. It *must* be dull for you, boxed up here, dependent on your aunt to get over the threshold, and she always was the most unpunctual person in the world except myself. Why don't you tell *me* when you want to go anywhere? I'd give up every engagement, as you know. Let's do something after luncheon. The Botanical Gardens—the Ancient Masters—even the South Kensington Museum! There, I'm game for anything you like!"

She could not help smiling, but it was a sad, wan smile, while she replied—

"You're very good, dear, and I'm a spoiled girl, I know; but, indeed, I'd rather stay at home, and so I'm sure would you."

"What have you settled about the concert to-morrow?" asked her father.

"Sent an excuse."

He pondered for a moment, and an expression of considerable annoyance crossed his face.

"I must get you out of town, Helen," said he. "The worst of it is I can't leave London myself just now—at least, for more than a day. If I could we'd go abroad. Paris is empty and hot; but we might get into Normandy, have a week at Trouville, and come back by Dieppe. Would you like *that?*"

"No, papa," she answered decidedly; but added, with hesitation, "if you could do without me, what I should like best would be to—to go back to Blackgrove at once."

"My *dear* Helen!" was all his astonishment allowed him to articulate. That a daughter of his should prefer the country to London, during the height of the season, seemed simply inexplicable.

"My *dear* papa!" repeated Helen, with another of those sad smiles. "I'll go to-morrow if you don't want me here. I wish I'd never come to London at all. The girls are so neglected when I'm away, and now we've no governess they get into all sorts of wild ways. I don't think they ought to be left so entirely to the servants. Lily writes me that she is up at five every morning to milk the cows. There's no harm in milking cows, but I think she would be better in bed, or learning her lessons. Indeed, papa, I should be much happier at Blackgrove than here. What do you think?"

What *did* he think? To a deeper mind than his it might have suggested itself that this yearning after home denoted some grievous injury, like that of a wounded animal making for its lair to lie down and die; but he took altogether a more practical and less romantic view of the case, attributing Helen's indisposition to stomach rather than heart.

"If you *really* wish it," said he. "Perhaps you are right. Early hours, in country air, will soon set you up again, and, of course, it's a great thing for the girls to have you with them. What a trouble they are, to be sure!"

Sir Henry always called his eldest "my daughter," his other female children "the girls," and his boy "the young one," as if the latter were a two-year-old, just about to be broke.

"Then I may go to-morrow?" exclaimed Helen, almost joyfully.

"Certainly, my dear," was the answer. "I'll take you down myself, sleep at Blackgrove, and come back next day by an afternoon train. I wish I could stay with you, but I can't."

"Of course it would be very nice for *me*," responded Miss Helen dutifully. "But you're not so much wanted, you know, when I'm there. While we're both away, things do get dreadfully 'to wrongs.' Oh! papa, I should like to go back and never leave Blackgrove again!"

With this domestic sentiment, much to his distress, astonishment, and even alarm, she hid her face in his breast, and began to cry heartily, emerging in a minute or so with a poor pretence of laughter, and an excuse that the hot weather was too much for her; as if a grown woman, with sound common sense and unusual self-command, ever cried because she was too hot. Sir Henry felt extremely uneasy. His varied experience of her sex had no doubt accustomed him to these ebullitions, but he had got into the habit of considering Helen superior to the rest, and it discomfited him sadly to find that she, too, could be weak, nervous, and, as he firmly believed, unhappy without a cause. He tried hard to persuade her to go to the French play that night, but Helen, wisely enough in my opinion considering the temperature, resisted firmly, and retired at ten o'clock.

Probably never in his life, except in a case of illness, had her father gone to bed before midnight. Lighting a cigar, he walked into the street and reflected which of his haunts he should visit to get rid of a couple of hours and shake off this feeling of anxiety and depression that had come over him about his daughter.

He was too pre-occupied for whist, and, truth to tell, even in his brightest moments, looked on that noble pastime as a study rather than a recreation. So he sauntered to St. James's Street, and in one club after another sought the distraction he required in vain. There were men enough in each, but all seemed engrossed with their own interests, their own affairs; greeting him, indeed, with the utmost courtesy, but volunteering no confidences, and inviting none in return. Most of them were younger than himself, and of his few contemporaries, one was lame from gout, another crippled with rheumatism, while a third volunteered the disheartening opinion that "it was time for fellows of *our* standing, my boy, to be in bed," rolling off while he thus delivered himself, with a hoarse, asthmatic, and unfeeling laugh. Sir Henry emerged on the pavement and shook his head.

"It's no use disguising it," he confided to his cigar, "I conclude I'm getting old; and the young ones are much more civil than they used to be, but not half so cordial. I liked them best when they slapped one on the back, asked one for a weed, and took all sorts of liberties. I suppose I must be an old fellow now, because nobody ever calls me one. It's 'Thank you, Sir Henry'—'With your permission, Sir Henry'—'Don't sit in the draught, Sir Henry;' and two years ago, they began to put me in the middle of the line partridge shooting, and to offer me a pony when the others walked the stubbles in the afternoon. I'm afraid I shall never hear a fellow say, 'Now then, Hal! Look alive, my boy!' again. If it's really come, there's no use in fighting against it. I've a great mind to give the whole thing up, and subside at once into an old fogie. I would, if it wasn't for Mrs. Lascelles —there's something taking about that woman, every now and then, she might almost make a fool of me still—I like her so the days she doesn't like *me*—the days she does, I don't care about her; so after all, what's the use? But she's fond of Helen. So was that other little black-eyed devil, Miss Ross. I wonder what has become of her; I wish I could find out. Everybody's fond of Helen. Ah! none of them are like *her*. If I could but see her thoroughly well and in good spirits again, I shouldn't care for these cursed money matters nor anything else. This place seems full enough. May as well go in."

Thus ruminating on his daughter, Sir Henry's feet had carried him almost unconsciously to the door of Pratt's, which popular resort was indeed crowded to overflowing, so that several members had established a merry and somewhat noisy conclave in the street.

Amongst these Picard was holding forth loudly, dispensing as usual his excellent cigars with the utmost liberality. Catching sight of Sir Henry, he detached himself from the circle, and taking the baronet by the arm, walked him back a few steps into St. James's Street.

"I came here on purpose to find you," said he, "and I wondered you were so late. I've good news! glorious news! Our shares are down again! I was in the City all day!"

Sir Henry swore, not loud but deep.

"Good news!" he answered. "I wonder what you'd call *bad!*"

"*Good* news," repeated Picard. "Buy more—go into it up to your neck. I'm dipped over-head. Listen, Sir Henry, this is a real good thing—there's not another man in London I would 'put on' but yourself; I'd private information from the other side last week. When the mail comes in, these Colorados will run up fifty, ay, seventy per cent.! Don't waste a moment, but grab all you can. It will set *me* on my legs, and I won't lose *my* footing again in a hurry, not if I know it! Shall you be at home to-morrow about luncheon time?"

"To-morrow?" said the other absently. "Not to-morrow. Must be at Blackgrove to-morrow—the next day certainly."

"Miss Hallaton is quite well I hope?" continued Picard, lifting his hat as if she were actually present.

"Quite well, thank you," answered Sir Henry, wishing him "good night;" but he was engrossed with his Colorados, and did not think of telling Picard that his daughter was going out of town.

CHAPTER XXVI.

IN SAMARIA.

The season, I have said, was wearing on, and, with waning summer, the heat increased to an intensity almost tropical. There are few parts of Europe where the atmosphere can be more suffocating than in London during dog-days, although while everybody goes about gasping, fainting, bewailing the temperature, nobody seems to dream of putting off ball, drum, dinner, or other festive gathering to a cooler date.

The July sun glared pitilessly down on square, street, and crescent, to be refracted with tenfold power from walls and pavements; the Park was a burnished waste, Mayfair an oven, and Belgravia a furnace. Cabmen plied in their shirt-sleeves, foot passengers put up their umbrellas, the water-carts disappeared altogether, and supply for once seemed inadequate to demand in the matter of beer.

If people drooped and languished in spacious drawing-rooms with sun-blinds, thorough draughts, fans, and all other appliances against the heat, what must that numerous class of our fellow-citizens have felt who live in stifling lodgings, stewing parlours over the kitchen and almost in the street, retired two-pair backs with eighteen inches of window, dusty carpets, heavy bed-furniture, and utter hopelessness of ventilation unaccompanied by showers of soot?

It is two o'clock in the day, the dinner-beer has been taken in and consumed, bare-armed artizans with short black pipes smoked out, are leaning and loitering at door-steps and window-ledge, doubtful whether to make holiday for the rest of the afternoon. A distant hum of children, like the drone of insects in a flower-garden, pervades the quarter; for the energy of childhood is irrepressible by atmospheric influences, but their hard-worked mothers are snatching a brief repose, and for a space, even their tongues are still. An omnibus has stopped at the corner public-house while the horses are watered, a coster-monger is fast asleep in his barrow by the road-side, and a drowsy, dreary torpor seems to pervade one of those narrow, tortuous streets that wind in an easterly direction from the Marlborough Road, S.W.

In the second floor of a shabby little house, a window stands as wide open as it can be propped by a bit of wood, and from that window, with a weary sigh, speaking volumes of patience, suffering, and sorrow, turns Miss Ross, to take her seat once more by the side of a low sofa-bed, and watch a toss of black curls, a little wan, pinched face, with a dull aching pain about her heart, that grows and strengthens as hope fades, and dies out, day by day. Poor Jin's own face has turned very white and thin too. Her features are sharpened, and the black eyes seem large, out of all proportion; yet never in the days gone by, when they flashed with coquetry, or sparkled with wit, did they possess so rare a charm, as the soft and tender lustre that shines in them now.

"It's cooler, dear, isn't it?" said she, pushing those dark curls off the pale little brow. "And mamma wasn't going to leave her pet—was she? Did Gustave think mamma could fly out at the window?" She tried to speak lightly, anything to woo a smile from the sick child, but he only replied by turning pettishly away, and burrowing his face in the pillow, while he murmured, "Not leave Johnnie—Johnnie wants his shoes—wants to be dressed and taken away." As he got weaker, he resisted and entirely repudiated the name of Gustave, and although he had nearly forgotten Mrs. Mole, would only acknowledge his own identity as the "Johnnie" who had been so christened in the cottage by the river-side.

The boy caught cold on that eventful evening when Miss Ross carried him off, and had never regained strength. The cold turned to low fever, and hour by hour, in those long broiling summer's days, he seemed to get gradually but surely weaker. He was fractious, though naturally sweet-tempered, restless without being in pain; there seemed no tangible organic malady, such as could be watched, fought against, overcome, but he drooped like a flower, and so drooping, well-nigh broke his mother's heart.

She never forgave herself, that the child had been exposed to rain on the evening she took him away. Arriving in London she at once sought this obscure locality, renting, indeed, the best rooms in the house, and sparing no expense for the comfort and convenience of her boy. By degrees, in addition to fears for his life, she had to face the anxiety of a waning purse, and the terrible consideration of what was to become of them both when her money was gone. The most skilful doctor in the neighbourhood was called in at a guinea a visit; very often he wouldn't take his guinea; very often there would have been none forthcoming, had he wanted it. For a time, they lived on Jin's wardrobe, her watch, her jewels, by degrees the sources of supply began to fail. Then she moved herself and her boy up-stairs. First, she had the whole second floor, then she gave up the other room, and, inhabiting one small apartment with her sick child, devoted to him her time, her energies, her whole existence, as she often thought, with sad, cold forebodings, in vain.

She starved, she pinched, she denied herself every luxury, almost every necessary, of life; but she never regretted what she had done, and she never lost courage.

"If Gustave gets well," she used to think, "I can work for him and me as I did before. If I can only struggle on till then, how happy I shall be. I shall have saved my boy. How could he but have been ruined under the care of that bad man? I shall have saved myself, for it is this poor patient angel who makes me good. And Frank, dear Frank! I shall have saved *you!* —you whom I loved better than myself! Ah! I have done well by you, and you will never know it. *Qu'est que ça fait?* It is finished, and there's an end of it. If my darling dies, what signifies anything? I shall soon die too! They will surely let me keep him in the next world. I who have had so little of him in this!"

Like the rest of us, she made for herself a future, all the brighter, no doubt, that the present seemed so cheerless and forlorn.

If the boy could only get well before her money was spent, if there was only enough left to defray the journey, she would carry him off with her to sunny France, there to live the old life, amongst the old scenes, in the old familiar way.

Her voice was still fresh, clear, and more powerful than ever; she need not surely seek long for an engagement, and under a false name, in those great southern towns, how was she to be traced or identified? She might defy Picard, she might even baffle the inquiries of Frank Vanguard, if, indeed, he loved her well enough to try and seek her out. The tears would come thick to her eyes while she pictured his sorrow and anxiety on her behalf, but she never wavered in her determination of keeping up an eternal barrier between them, and of devoting her whole existence henceforth to her child. Had she known how Frank accepted her loss with an uncomplaining resignation, very far short of despair, waking up, as it were, from a dream, with a feeling that, after all, things might have been worse, it is possible she would have shown less resolution; but believing *him* to be inconsolable, she felt herself impracticable and pitiless as adamant. Who shall say how far such dreams helped her to bear the nursing, the watching, the fatigue, the heavy anxious days, the long, weary hours of those sultry, sleepless nights?

Except to go for medicine, for arrowroot, or to summon the doctor on some fresh alarm, Jin never stirred across the threshold, nor drew a breath of fresher air than could be obtained at the window of the sick-chamber.

Amongst other womanly trinkets and trifles, she had a large fan left, of small money value, but admirably adapted to its purpose. Under the judicious application of this instrument, the child gradually became cooler and less feverish. At length, with a few drowsy murmurs, in which "Mamma" and "Moley" were mixed up unintelligibly, the empty phial that had served him for a toy dropped from his poor little wasted fingers, and he went to sleep. Then Jin, bethinking her that the phial must be refilled according to medical directions, sought out the prescription, caught up her bonnet and parasol, drew on her last pair of gloves, and stole downstairs, leaving the door ajar, while impressing on the maid-of-all-work that she must peep in every five minutes to see if the little invalid were still asleep; she herself would not be gone a quarter of an hour.

I don't care how hard a woman is worked, I never knew one yet but could make time to look after a child. From the little girl of three, who carries a doll as big as herself, to the aged dame of threescore, who has been dandling children and children's children all her life, not one of the sex but handles an infant with instinctive dexterity, such as no amount of mere practice could ensure. Even the sourest old maid may be entrusted with a baby; nor is there the slightest fear that she will crease it, drop it, or carry it upside down. The poor drudge who answered Jin's summons with grimy hands and unwashed face, would have liked nothing better than to tend Gustave morning, noon, and night. She only hoped Miss Ross would stay out the whole afternoon.

It was a relief to emerge from the narrow street, and, after five minutes' walk, to cross the Fulham Road. Even that suburban thoroughfare seemed to glitter with life and motion after the gloomy sick-room, and the dull monotony on which its single window looked out. But Jin had no time to spare, and was speedily in the chemist's shop waiting for her prescription to be made up.

The young man behind the counter, clean, curly, smug, and white-handed, was affable and considerate. "Take a seat, miss," said he, pointing to a high cane chair. "You seem fatigued like, and faint. The weather, miss, is uncommon hot this season. Very trying to some constitutions. Directly, miss. Certainly. Quite a simple prescription. Shall be made up in five minutes. Address on the phial, I see. Allow me to send it for you."

Poor Jin, faint and weak from watching and exhaustion, protested feebly against this arrangement; glad to sit down, nevertheless, for her knees knocked together, and she trembled from top to toe.

A dreadful misgiving came across her of what was to be done if she should fall ill too; but Jin was not a nervous person, and felt almost capable of keeping off bodily disorder by a strong effort of the will.

In the meantime, the young man, hiding his curly head first in one drawer, then in another, brayed certain mysterious compounds in a mortar, and, dissolving the nauseous mixture, poured it into a fresh bottle, packing the whole carefully in paper, with string and sealing-wax, not hand-ing it to Miss Ross till, in spite of her impatience, he had copied, in fair and legible writing, the whole label attached to the discarded vessel. This last bore no name, but on it were minute directions as to how the draught must be taken, and the address at which it was to be left.

There was less to pay than she expected; but she had not intended to be absent from her boy so long, and, seizing the packet with impatience, dashed out of the shop to hurry home.

There was no shady side of the street. An afternoon sun beat fiercely on her raven hair, not in the least protected by the wisp of lace, with a leaf in it, that constituted her bonnet. She had slept but little in the last forty-eight hours, and eaten less. Crossing the Fulham Road, everything seemed to turn round with her; the roar, as of a thousand carriages, surged in her ears. She thought she was being run over, and, making an effort to reach the kerbstone, staggered, tripped, and fell.

A very handsome horse, with too much plating on his harness, was pulled hard on his haunches;

a brougham, painted and varnished like a new toy, stood still with a jerk, and a woman's voice from the interior exclaimed, in high accents of condemnation and command—

"Why don't you stop, you infernal idiot? You've knocked the woman down, and now you want to drive over her!"

Kate Cremorne habitually jumped at conclusions. On the present occasion she jumped also out of her carriage, with exceeding promptitude, and lifted Miss Ross off the ground almost before the bystanders knew the latter had fallen. Glancing at the packet still clutched tightly in her hand, she summoned a benevolent drayman to the rescue, and, with the assistance of that worthy, who testified unqualified approval of the whole proceeding, and called both ladies "pretty dears" more than once during its performance, placed the poor drooping sufferer in the carriage, and directed her groom to drive without delay—"like smoke," I am afraid, was the expression she used—to the address she had so quickly mastered. Then, and not till then, she produced smelling-bottle, fan, and laced handkerchief to restore her charge to consciousness.

In Brompton, you see, as in Samaria of old, are to be found those who bear in mind the great parable that has made the name of Samaritan synonymous with the most Christian-like of all Christian virtues.

Had Kate "passed on, on the other side," she would not have spoiled an extremely expensive morning-dress; she would not have been too late for one of the fastest and liveliest of Richmond dinner-parties; she would not have missed the man of all others in London who most wished to meet *her*. But to none of these did she give a thought nor a sigh while she bathed Jin's pale temples with eau-de-cologne, and rested the dark drooping head on her snowy bosom, pressing it to her own warm, wilful, reckless, restless heart.

It was not till they reached her remote and shabby refuge, that Miss Ross came thoroughly to herself; but even then she looked so white and ill, that Kate would not hear of leaving her, but insisted on helping her up-stairs, and taking command at once as superintendent, head-nurse, in short, captain-general of the whole establishment.

Living, so to speak, on the border-land between good and bad society, Kate Cremorne knew Miss Ross perfectly well by sight, though Miss Ross did not know Kate Cremorne. The shrewd, practical, world-experienced girl saw the whole affair at a glance. Through her keen intellect flashed a history of perfidy, sorrow, penury, a scrape, a scandal, a reduced lady, and a half-acted romance. She had sufficient delicacy to conceal her recognition of Miss Ross; but it was Kate's nature to take the lead in whatever position she was placed, and it would not have been her had she failed to make everything airy and comfortable about the sufferer in ten minutes.

She dismissed her brougham, much to the admiration of the public, with directions to return in an hour; she sent the maid out for soup, and the landlady for wine; she did not even forget to order some cut flowers; she rustled up and down-stairs without waking Johnnie; she insisted on the front room, fortunately unoccupied, being at once got ready for Miss Ross, producing that best of references—a little *porte-monnaie*, with sovereigns in it. She took off her bonnet, made herself completely at home, kissed the sleeping child, and won the hearts of the people of the house almost ere Jin had thoroughly opened her eyes; and long before the brougham returned to carry her away she had put the invalid to bed, given her a basin of soup, with a glass of port wine in it, and was soothing her off to sleep, gently and quietly as a mother hushes a baby.

"You want rest, dear," she whispered, smoothing the pillow with her strong white hand. "I won't leave you till you're as sound as that beautiful boy in the next room. Then I'll go and sit with him till you wake, and after that I needn't bother you any more, unless you'll let me come and see you the first thing to-morrow morning."

Jin smiled faintly, and opened her eyes.

"I don't know who you are," she whispered; "but you're the only kind-hearted woman I ever met in my life, except one. God bless you!"

Then her head sank back, and every nerve seemed to relax in the overpowering motionless sleep of utter exhaustion.

But Kate, watching her, looked very grave and thoughtful. She had not been used to blessings. Perhaps in her whole past she had never earned one so true and heartfelt before. The sensation was strange, almost oppressive, opening up a new series of hopes, feelings, interests, and reflections, with certain wistful misgivings, that she, fair, fast, flighty Kate Cremorne had hitherto mistaken the chief objects of existence, wasted her life, and thrown herself away.

CHAPTER XXVII.

A HOUSEHOLD KATE.

"WHAT an odd girl you are, Kate!" said Mrs. Battersea, as the sisters sat at breakfast next morning in their pretty suburban garden, with a table drawn under the acacia-tree, and as many birds, roses, and strawberries about them as if they were a hundred miles from London. "You lost the best chance yesterday that ever woman had, and all because you couldn't be in time for a train. My dear, I don't often scold; but it *does* provoke me to see you throw yourself away. I begin to think you'll never *settle*, Kate. You're worse than I was; you're worse than I am *now!*"

"That's a bad state of things," answered Kate saucily. "I shouldn't have thought it possible. But what's the use of settling, Auntie?" The elder sister had once been taken for the younger's aunt, and the nickname had stuck to her. "You talk as if I was some sort of mess on a kitchen hob. Why *should* I settle, and why do you stir me up? I'm very nice as I am."

"So Mr. Goldthred seems to think!" answered her sister; "and if you'd only been with us yesterday, you'd have had him to yourself the whole afternoon. I'm sure he was disappointed; and to see the barefaced way that odious little Rosie made up to him was quite sickening! Kate—Kate—don't you want an establishment of your own?"

"What's the good?" replied the other, dipping a bit of cake in her coffee. "I'm very happy as I am—

'O give me back my hollow tree,
My crust of bread, and liberty!'

Freedom and simplicity, say I; communism, equality, and fraternity!"

"Kate, you're talking nonsense," pursued

Mrs. Battersea. "Nature never intended *you* for a country-mouse, and there's no such thing as equality, fraternity, and all that. Talk of men being brothers! Bosh! Men are intended for husbands, only you must strike while the iron's hot. They harden sadly if they're allowed to get cool. Oh, Kate! I do wish you'd been with us yesterday! We went on the river after dinner. There was a moon, and everything!"

"Did you have a good dinner?" asked Kate saucily.

"Of course we had," said the other. "But that's nothing to the purpose. I tell you the whole party were paired off, except Goldie; and he went about like a poor disconsolate bird in a frost. Rosie tried hard for him; but he wouldn't look at her; and, besides, she'd got her own admirer. I tell you, if you'd only been on the spot, the whole thing might have been settled."

"Who was there for *you?*" inquired Miss Kate, with mischievous eyes and a ripe cherry in her mouth, not much redder than the lips against which it bobbed.

"Why the Colonel, naturally," answered Mrs. Battersea. "You knew that quite well, so what's the use of asking? I shall 'shunt' the Colonel, Kate, after Goodwood, he's getting so *very* grey, and it looks really ridiculous amongst young people, like our party yesterday."

"By all means," assented Kate. "And who's to replace him? Not that half-bred American, Mr. Picard, I hope. Trust me, Aunty; I have predatory instincts, and they never deceive me. That man is an adventurer; he's not a gentleman. Look at him by the others: you see it at once."

Mrs. Battersea burst out laughing.

"Well done, Kate! This is indeed teaching your grandmother. Do you think I'm still too young to run alone? I ought to be flattered, and I *am*. Don't you trouble your head about Picard and me. He's useful for the present. When I've done with him, you may be pretty sure I shall drop him. Now tell me, dear, what the temptation was that kept you away all yesterday, and deprived our party, as the Colonel said, of the 'bonniest bud in the bouquet.'"

"I'd an adventure," enunciated Kate solemnly.

"Was he good looking?" exclaimed Mrs. Battersea.

"*Very!*" answered Kate. "But I only saw him asleep. He had the blackest curls and the longest eyelashes I ever beheld on man or woman. Such a darling, Auntie! But though I kissed him without disturbing him one bit, I don't suppose he'll ever pay me the gloves I'm entitled to by all the rules of racing."

Mrs. Battersea looked puzzled.

"What *do* you mean?" said she. "I never can quite make you out when you're in these wild moods. I hope you haven't been getting into mischief. Your spirits run away with you so, I ought never to let you out of my sight."

Kate laughed merrily.

"It's not much of a scrape this time," she answered, "nor much of a lark neither. I paid a morning visit in a fashionable quarter, and was detained longer than I anticipated, that's all. What should you say if I'd found something 'stolen or strayed, lost or mislaid;' something not actually advertised, but that would be worth 'a reward' all the same, if I was to produce it at one or two places I know in London, not to mention the cavalry barracks at Windsor?"

"You speak in parables," said the other, crumbling up bread and cream for her parrot. "When you come down to plain English and common sense, I shall be able to understand."

"I've found Miss Ross!" Kate closed her pretty lips so tight after this startling information that the cherry snapped off at its stalk, and bobbed into her coffee-cup.

"You've found Miss Ross!" repeated her sister, in accents of the utmost astonishment. "Well, it's *too* bad of Captain Vanguard; quite too bad, I must say! And, Kate, I won't have you getting mixed up with that kind of thing. Recollect we can scarcely hold our own where we are; and although, for myself, I think respectable society rather *slow*, I don't want you to make the mistakes I did. Never set the world at defiance, my dear; it don't answer. You may humbug people to any extent, but they won't stand being bullied! Don't go near her again, Kate, I beg. Somebody is sure to see you."

"Captain Vanguard has no more to do with it than *you* have," retorted Miss Cremorne, ignoring her sister's late monitions and reverting to the first count in the indictment. "Why can you never let him alone? Tell me, Auntie, once for all, what's this grudge of yours against Frank? Poor thing! How has it affronted its aunt?"

Mrs. Battersea looked grave.

"He'll never have a chance of affronting *me*, Kate, unless he does it through *you*. He hangs about here a great deal too much. He haunts the places we go to like a ghost; and he *looks* like a ghost besides, for he has lost his colour, grown very silent, and never smiles. I say nothing, but——"

"You *think* a great deal, no doubt," replied

her sister. "You think wrong this time, though, if you fancy I care two straws about Frank, or Frank about *me*. He *was* pleasant enough, I grant you; but now that he's got sad, and quiet, and stupidish, he bores me. You ought to know my tastes better than most people, dear. You may be pretty sure one of your languishing swains has very little chance. I hate long stories, long memories, long sighs, and long faces. If people like one, they should make one happy.—

'When Love is kind,
  Lightsome, and free,
Love's sure to find
  Welcome from me,
But if Love brings
  Heart-ache or pang,
Tears, or such things,
  Love may go hang!'

"Which only proves you were never in earnest, Kate," answered the elder woman; adding, with a sigh, "So much the better for *you*."

Perhaps Mrs. Battersea was thinking of a time long before she met the late Major Battersea, a time when Kate was a little toddling thing, with fat legs, chubby arms, and the manners of a confirmed and shameless flirt; a time when the sands of the Isle of Wight borrowed a golden gleam from that light which so irradiates the present to leave behind it such grim, ghostly shadows on the past; when the waves sang soft sweet music, softer, sweeter, for the whisper that stole through the drowsy wash and murmur of the tide,—sadder, too, for an instinct that warns the human heart how they will make the same melodious moan, unchanged, unpitying, after they have closed over its happiness for ever; when morning was a vision of hope, and evening a dream of peace, and all day long a waking reality of happiness, because of a straw hat, a sun-burned face, and a light laugh. Perhaps she was contrasting a certain frank, innocent, loving girl, trusting and true-hearted, with the woman of after years, marred and warped by her first disappointment, carrying war on bravely in the enemy's country, but aching still under all her armour of pride and indifference, with the dull pain of that first grievous wound.

"So much the better for me," repeated Kate thankfully. "You would have said so, indeed, if you could have seen that poor thing yesterday. Pale, worn, dejected, and, my dear, so very badly dressed! I declare I hardly knew her again, and I used to think, for quite a dark beauty, she was the best-looking woman in London. Do you suppose, Auntie, there really *is* such a thing as a broken heart, or is it all nonsense and what they put in novels, and poems, and things? It must hurt horribly if there is!"

"Some people mind it more than others," answered her sister. "Let us be thankful, Kate, that you and I are not of the caring sort. But what do you suppose has brought Miss Ross to this pass? She used to be one of your regular high-fliers. Went to Court, I fancy, and all the rest of it. And how do you know your precious Frank Vanguard hadn't a finger in the pie?"

"Because I *do* know," affirmed Miss Kate. "You never saw such a place as she was living in; and I got everything out of the people in the house before I had been there ten minutes."

"I can easily believe it," said her sister. "As usual, taking up another's business and neglecting your own."

"But I mean to make it my own," protested Kate. "You would have been as keen about it as I am if you had seen the poor thing huddled up in her refuge like a frightened cat in a corner. Table on three legs, chairs falling to pieces, such a small room, such stuffy furniture, and you might have written your name in dust on everything. Even her gown was all frayed at the skirt, and there wasn't another in the wardrobe, for I peeped in to see. I shall be off again directly after breakfast, and perhaps to-day I may worm something out of her, and get her to let me help her in earnest, you know. How sad, Auntie, to come to such a pass! Fancy not having enough to eat, and only one gown to put on!"

"But the child," persisted Mrs. Battersea, "the child couldn't have come there by chance. Kate, I wish you'd let it all alone."

"The child was as clean as a new pin,"

answered Miss Cremorne. "There was everything he could want arranged for him as nicely as if he was a little Emperor! That's why I'm sure she's his mother. I don't care if she's his *grandmother* a hundred times over. I'll stick by her now through this mess, whatever it is. I've gone in for it, and I'll see it out! I'll charter a Hansom, though; I won't take the brougham, it makes people stare."

Mrs. Battersea pondered, and the parrot, waiting for his breakfast, shrieked hideously.

"Don't you think I'm right?" asked the impatient girl.

"I know you won't be stopped," answered the other, "right or wrong. But were I in your place I should certainly not interfere. If Captain Vanguard has anything to do with the business, I cannot see what good will come of your mixing yourself up in it. Frank's very good-looking, I grant you, and pleasanter company than half the men we meet; but I don't suppose he really cares two pins for anything but his horses; and as for heart, my dear Kate, these guardsmen are all alike—they throw the article systematically away before their moustache is grown, and find they get on very much better without it afterwards."

"They may throw them about till they're tired," answered Kate. "They'll have to wait a long time before I stoop to pick one up, Auntie. I never saw the man yet that was worth crossing the street for, after a shower. Did you?"

"*One*, Kate," said Mrs. Battersea, "long ago. I'd have gone into the Serpentine, up to my neck at least, for *him*."

"Why didn't you?" asked the other. "What has become of him?"

"He never asked me," replied Mrs. Battersea, with something of a tremble in her voice. "I thought I was so sure of him, I could get him back at any time, and one fine morning I pulled my thread the least thing too hard, and it broke. I saw him the other day, Kate, quite by accident. He hasn't forgiven, for all the years that are past,—and, though it seems ridiculous, I haven't forgotten."

"Never say die! Auntie," laughed the girl. "You've plenty of admirers left!"

"Plenty!" said Mrs. Battersea; "but they're not the real stuff. They're like cheap dresses, my dear, look well enough while they're new, but when they've been worn a little, particularly in bad weather, they go all to pieces."

"The Colonel, for instance," observed Kate. "He's so threadbare now, I don't think he'll even make up into patch-work or even pen-wipers. Auntie, you're very hard upon the Colonel, and I do believe he's fond of you."

"So he ought to be," answered Mrs. Battersea. "But let the Colonel alone, Kate, and take my advice. If you find a man who really likes you better than his dinner, his Derby, his covert-shooting, or his best horse, don't stop to consider whether he is romantic, and popular, and admired. Make up your mind at once. Take him frankly, unless you absolutely hate the creature. Stand by him honestly, and never throw him over. When you're as old as I am you'll be glad you followed my advice."

"I must first *catch* my hare," replied Miss Kate, rising from the table; "and then there's an end of the excitement, the ups-and-downs, the ins-and-outs, the falls and fences, in short, all the fun of the hunt. Well, who knows? Perhaps my time may come, like another's.

'Puis ce que ça doit se tirer au sort.'

But meanwhile I do very well as I am, and when I've found my master it will be quite soon enough to 'knuckle down' and give in. So now I'm off to my poor sick bird, to nurse her chick, and sleek her feathers, and put to rights her untidy little nest."

Accordingly, in less than ten minutes Miss Cremorne emerged into the sunshine, as well-looking and as well-dressed a young lady as could be seen treading the pavement of any street in London. A butcher's boy, with tray on shoulder, stopped short in his whistle to look after her, transported with admiration. A young man from the country stood stock-still under the very pole of an omnibus, and grinned his approval open-mouthed; while an old gentleman, who ought to have known better, crossed the muddiest part of the street, and affected great interest in an upholsterer's window, to get one more look at her pretty face as she tripped past. The very cabman whom she signalled off the rank forbore to overcharge her, and came down officiously from the perch of his Hansom to keep her dress off the wheel when she alighted, wondering the while at the homely exterior of the dwelling in which this vision of beauty disappeared.

"It's a queer start!" soliloquized that worthy in his own expressive vernacular; "and females, as a general rule, is up to all sorts of games. But she ain't one of that sort, she ain't. Blessed if she don't look as bold as Britannia, the beauty! and as h'innocent as a nosegay all the while!"

CHAPTER XXVIII.

"TENDER AND TRUE."

According to promise, Picard called on Sir Henry at his house in town, and was fortunate enough to find the baronet at home, but being ushered into a room on the ground-floor, smelling strongly of tobacco-smoke, his heart misgave him that he was about to fail in the chief object of his visit, and that Helen had gone out. He was further discomfited by his host's information that she was at Blackgrove, with no intention of returning to London till next spring. The adventurer's brow clouded. He had but little time for delay, and felt, to use his own expression, that the moment had arrived when he must force the running, come with a rush, and win on the post the best way he could.

Affecting, therefore, an air of deep concern, he sat himself down opposite Sir Henry, who, wrapped in velvet, occupied the easiest of chairs, with a French novel on his knee, and began to apologise for disturbing him.

"But I wanted to see you," said Picard, in a more subdued tone than usual, "because, in trying to do you a good turn, I've got you into a mess. It is fortunate you are a man of position, and—and—of means, Sir Henry, so that this is a matter of mere temporary inconvenience, but it is equally distressing to me, I assure you, just the same."

"What do you mean?" said Sir Henry, turning pale, while the French novel fluttered to his feet.

"Simply, that in following my lead about those shares I fear you have come to grief. Not to the extent I have, of course, but still enough to make you very shy of taking my advice in money-matters again. I shall pull through myself, eventually, well enough; but I had rather lose every shilling I possess than that a friend of mine should sustain injury by my advice or example."

The nobility of this sentiment was thrown away on Sir Henry, who swore an ugly oath, and for a moment seemed in danger of losing his habitual self-command.

"Why, you told me those cursed Colorados were a *certainty!*" he exclaimed; "'a clear gain of fifty per cent.,' were your very words, no questions asked, and no risk to run. You're not a baby, my good fellow! Who was it that took *you* in, I should like to know? He must have his wits about him, that gentleman!"

"I can only repeat I did everything for the best," answered Picard loftily. "I trust you were not in it very deep!"

"*Deep!*" growled the baronet. "I don't know what you call *deep*. I counted on those cursed shares to pay off all my pressing liabilities, and to square me with *you* in particular. Now that one card has gone the whole house will tumble down, of course. It's always the way. Hang it, Picard! you oughtn't to have been so cock-sure, man. Well, it's no use talking. I'm simply floored, that's all; and how I'm to be picked up *this* time beats my comprehension altogether."

"You have friends, Sir Henry," said Picard. "Plenty of them."

"Plenty of them!" echoed Sir Henry. "Staunch friends and true, who would dine with me, bet with me, shoot with me, nay, some of whom would even back me up in a row, or pull for me while hounds were running if I got a fall, but who would see me d——d before they lent me a shilling, or put their names to a bill for eighteen pence."

"That may be true enough with some of your swell acquaintance," replied Picard, "but you mustn't lump us all in together and ticket us 'rotten.' I myself am ready, now, this moment, to do my utmost to assist you. Sir Henry, I am a real friend."

"If you know my liabilities, by Heaven you are!" exclaimed the baronet, with a sarcastic grin.

"I don't care a cent for your liabilities!" said the other, as indeed he might safely say; and perhaps Sir Henry's knowledge of the world attributed this generosity to the recklessness of one who had nothing to lose. "I don't care what they are, I'll see you through them. I am your friend—your true friend—Sir Henry—I am more than a friend. The dearest wish of my heart is to be in the same boat with yourself and your family, sink or swim."

In an instant, the baronet's whole demeanour changed to one of studied and even guarded courtesy. He rose from his chair, stood with his back to the empty fire-place, and inclined politely to his visitor.

"I do not quite understand," said he. "Pray explain."

Picard hesitated. There was something embarrassing in the other's attitude. It combined civility, defiance, vigilance, all the ingredients, indeed, of an armed neutrality. At last he got out the words, "Your daughter, Sir Henry—Miss Hallaton."

"Stop a moment," interrupted the baronet, still in those guarded, courteous tones; "how *can* my daughter be concerned in our present business?"

"Simply," answered the other, fairly driven into a corner, "that I had meant—that I had intended—in short, that I had hoped you might be induced to entertain—I mean, to listen favourably. Hang it! Sir Henry, I am devotedly attached to your daughter—there!"

Sir Henry drew himself up. "You do Miss Hallaton a great honour," said he, very stiffly, "and one I beg to decline most distinctly on her behalf. This is a subject which admits of no further discussion between you and me."

"Are you in earnest?" exclaimed Picard fiercely. "Do you know what you are doing? Have you counted the cost of making me your enemy? Sir Henry, you must surely have lost your head or your temper?"

"Neither, I assure you," answered the other, with provoking calmness; adding, while he laid his hand on the bell-pull—"May I offer you a glass of sherry, and—and—*bitters*, before you go?"

For the life of him, he could not resist a sarcastic emphasis, while he named that wholesome tonic, nor could he help smiling, as Picard, losing all self-control, flung out of the room, with no more courteous leave-taking than a consignment of the proffered refreshment to a temperature where it would have proved acceptable in the highest degree.

But no sooner had the street-door closed on his visitor, than Sir Henry shook himself, as it were, out of a life's lethargy, and seemed to become a new man. It was his nature to rise against a difficulty; and, although he had never before had such a souse in the cold waters of adversity, he felt braced and strengthened by the plunge. He sat down at once to his writing-table, and immersed himself in calculations as to liabilities, and means of meeting them. Ruin stared him in the face. He was convinced he had nothing to hope from Picard's forbearance, with whom he was inextricably mixed up in money matters.

He saw clearly that the latter would use every legal engine in his power to further his revenge; yet Sir Henry's courage failed him not a jot, and he only cursed the scoundrel's impudence in thinking himself good enough for Helen, vowing the while he would be a match for them all, and fight through yet.

Then he wrote many letters to solicitors, money-lenders, and private friends; amongst others, one to Helen, and one to Mrs. Lascelles. It is with this last alone we have to do.

That lady is sitting, somewhat disconsolate and lonely, in the pretty boudoir at No. 40. The bullfinch is moulting, and sulky in the extreme; the pug has been dismissed for the only misdemeanour of which he is ever guilty—indigestion, followed by sickness; the post has just brought Sir Henry Hallaton's letter; Mrs. Lascelles is dissolved in tears; and Goldthred, who has not been near her for a fortnight, is suddenly announced.

All the morning, all the drive hither in a Hansom cab, all the way up-stairs, he has been revolving how he can best carry out Kate Cremorne's precept—"Il faut se faire valoir;" but at the top step the loyalty of a true, disinterested love asserts itself, and he would fain fall prone at the feet of his mistress, bidding her trample him in the dust if she had a mind.

Seeing her in tears, he turned hot and cold, dropped his hat, knocked down a spidery table in trying to recover it, and finally shook hands with the woman he loved stiffly and pompously, as if she had been his bitterest enemy.

The grasp of her hand too seemed less cordial, her manner less kindly than usual. Goldthred, who had yet to learn that the fortress never mans its walls with so much menace as on the eve of surrender, felt chilled, dispirited, even hurt; but, because of her distress, staunch and unwavering to the backbone.

"You find me very unhappy," said she, drying her eyes (gently, so as not to make them unbecomingly red). "Why have you never been to see me?"

This, turning on him abruptly, and with a

degree of displeasure that ought to have raised his highest hopes.

"I've been away," he stammered, "in the North on business. I—I didn't know you wanted me."

"Oh, it's not *that!*" she answered pettishly. "Of course, one can't expect people to put off business, or pleasure, or anything else for the sake of their friends. What's the *use* of friends? What's the use of caring for anything or anybody? I wish I didn't. I shouldn't be so upset now!"

In his entire participation of her sorrow, he quite lost his own embarrassment.

"Can I do anything?" he exclaimed. "There's the *will*, you know, even if there isn't the power."

"Nothing, that I can see," she answered drearily. "Here's a letter from Sir Henry Hallaton. They're completely ruined, he tells me; a regular smash! What is to become of them? I'm so wretched, particularly about Helen."

She put her handkerchief to her face once more, but watched her listener narrowly, nevertheless. It did not escape her that his countenance changed and fell, as if he had been stung.

He recovered himself bravely, though.

"That is distressing enough," said he, "and sounds a bad business, no doubt. Still, it is only a question of money, I suppose. It might have been worse."

"Worse!" she repeated, with impatience. "I don't see how. From what he says, it seems they won't have a roof to cover them—hardly bread to eat! And what can I do for him? I can't pay off his mortgages, and buy him back Blackgrove, as if it was a baby-house. It *does* seem so hard! It makes me hate everything and everybody!"

Goldthred's only reply to this rational sentiment was to rise from his chair, button his coat, and place himself in a determined attitude on the hearth-rug.

"You seem very miserable," said he; and the man's voice was so changed that she started as if a stranger had come into the room. "I think I can understand why—no, don't explain anything, Mrs. Lascelles, but listen to me—you are unhappy. To the best of my power I will help you. Somebody that you—well—that you like very much is in difficulties. If I can extricate him, I will. You needn't hate everything or everybody any longer," he added, with rather a sad smile; "and you may believe that, though people do not put off their business nor their pleasure for them, they can sometimes sacrifice their interests to their friends."

How noble he seemed standing there—so kind, so good, so utterly unselfish and true! How she loved him! She had long guessed it. She knew it too surely now. Yet she could not forbear taking the last arrow from her quiver, and sending it home to his honest, unsuspecting heart.

"It is very kind of you, Mr. Goldthred," said she, "to speak as you do, particularly as you always mean what you say; but, though I often fancied you liked her, I had no idea your attachment to Miss Hallaton was so strong as all that!"

He turned very pale, and stooped over the moulting bullfinch, without speaking; then raised his head, looking—as she had never seen him look before—resolved, even stern, thoughtful, saddened, yet not the least unkind; and the voice, that had trembled awhile ago, was firm and decided now.

"If you are joking, Mrs. Lascelles," said he, "the jest is unworthy of *you*, and unfair on *me*. If you really think what you say, it is time you were undeceived. Miss Hallaton is no more to me than a young lady in whom you take an interest. For her father I am prepared to make any sacrifice, because I think you—Mrs. Lascelles, will you forgive what I am going to say?"

"I don't know," she answered, smiling very brightly, considering that the tears still glittered in her eyes. "I might be more deeply offended than you suppose. What if you were going to say you think I am in love with Sir Henry Hallaton?"

"I think you *are* in love with Sir Henry Hallaton," he repeated very gravely. "I think your happiness has long been dependent on his society. I think you would marry him to-morrow if he asked you. I think he would ask you to-day if his position admitted of it. I do not live a great deal in the world, Mrs. Lascelles, and I daresay I am rather dull in a general way; but the stupidest people can see things that affect their interests or their happiness; and I have often watched every word and look of yours, when you thought perhaps I had no more perception, no more feeling, than that marble chimney-piece. Sometimes with a sore heart enough; but that is all over now! Ought I to have told you long ago, or ought I to have held my tongue for ever? I don't know; but I need not tell you now, that from the day Mr. Groves introduced me to you, at the Thames Regatta—I daresay you've forgotten all about it—I have admired you, and—and—cared for you more than anything in the world. You're too bright and too beautiful and too good for me, I know; but that don't prevent my wanting to see you happy, and happy you *shall* be, Mrs. Lascelles, if everything I can do has the power to make you so!"

His voice may have failed him somewhat during this simple little declaration, but seemed steady enough when he finished; and it could not, therefore, have been from sympathy with his emotion that the tears were again rising fast to his listener's blue eyes.

"I remember it perfectly," she sobbed. "You were talking to a fat woman in a hideous yellow gown. Why do you say I don't?"

"Remember what?" he asked innocently, not being quite conversant with a manœuvre much practised by ladies in difficulties, and similar to that resource which is termed in the prize-ring "sparring for wind."

"Why, the first time I met you," she answered. "You're not the only person who has a memory and feelings and all that. I know you must think me a brute, and so I am; but still, I'm not quite a woman of stone!"

"I have told you what I think of you," said he very quietly. "Now tell me what I can do for you, and *him.*"

"Do you mean," she asked, peeping slyly out of her little useless handkerchief, "that you would actually give me up to somebody else, and part with your *money*, which is always a criterion of sincerity, for such an object? Mr. Goldthred, is *that* what you call love?"

"I only want you to be happy," said he. "I don't understand much about love and flirtation; and these things people make such a talk about. I want to see you happy. No, not that; for I should avoid seeing you, at least just at first; but I should like to *know* you were happy, and that it was my doing."

He turned, and leaned his elbows on the chimney-piece, not to look in the glass; for his face was buried in his hands, so that she had some difficulty in attracting his attention. It was not a romantic action; but she gave a gentle pull at his coat-tails.

"You *can* make me happy," she whispered,

with a deep and very becoming blush. "I don't think it will be at all inconvenient or unpleasant to you, only—only—you know I can't exactly suggest it first."

He turned as if he was shot. With white face and parted lips, never man looked more astonished, while he gasped out—

"And you wouldn't marry Sir Henry Halaton?"

She shook her head with a very bewitching smile.

"And you *would* marry me?" he continued, hardly daring to believe it was not all a dream.

"You've never asked me," was the reply; but he was on the sofa at her side by this time, whispering his answer so closely in her ear, that I doubt if either heard it, while both knew pretty well what it meant; and though their subsequent conversation was carried on in a strange mixture of broken sentences, irrational expressions, and idiotic dumb show, it took less than ten minutes to arrive at a definite conclusion, entailing on Goldthred the necessity of immediate correspondence with his nearest relatives, and a visit to Doctors' Commons at no far distant date.

But, happy as he felt, breathing elixir, treading upon air, while walking home to dress for dinner, he found time for the purchase of such a beautiful fan as can hardly be got for money, and sent it forthwith to Kate Cremorne, with the following line written in pencil on his card—*Il faut se faire valoir.*

CHAPTER XXIX.

DAYBREAK.

It is only your cubs bred last season, not yet many months emancipated from the tender authority of the vixen, that hang to their homes, and run circling round the covert when disturbed by the diligence of their natural enemy, the hound. An old fox is a wild fox; and no sooner does he recognise the mellow note of the huntsman's cheer, the crack of the first whip's ponderous thong, than he is on foot and away, lively as a lark, with a defiant whisk of his brush, that means seven or eight miles as the crow flies, the exercise of all his speed during the chase, and all his craft to beat you at the finish. If you would have that brush on your chimney-piece, that sharp little nose on your kennel door, you must be pretty quick after him, for he wastes not a moment in hesitation, facing the open resolutely for his haven, crossing the fields like an arrow, wriggling through the fences like an eel.

Sir Henry Hallaton had been too often hunted not to take alarm at the first intelligence of real danger, therefore it was that he put the Channel between himself and his creditors without delay, knowing well from experience that a man never makes such good terms as when out of his enemy's reach; and so, trusting in the chapter of accidents which had often befriended him, smoked his cigar tranquilly in a pleasant little French town, while his family, his servants, his tradesmen, everybody connected with him, were paying, in distress, discomfort, and anxiety, the penalties this self-indulgent gentleman had incurred for his own gratification.

There could scarcely have been a greater contrast than the position of father and daughter when the crash first came.

Sir Henry lived in cheerful apartments, dined

at a tolerable *table-d'hôte*, sipped a *petit vin de Bordeaux* that always agreed with him, smoked good cigars, and frequented a social circle, not very distinguished, nor indeed very respectable, but in which, with his fatal facility of getting into mischief, he found himself always welcome and always amused.

When his letters were written and posted, he felt without a care in the world for the rest of the day, and positively looked younger and fresher in his exile than at any time during the last five years, though there was an execution in the house at Blackgrove, and he had not a shilling to his name.

Helen, on the contrary, found herself beset with every kind of annoyance and difficulty, from the black looks of a principal creditor to the loud reproaches of a discharged scullery-maid. Her father indeed wrote her full and explicit directions what to do in the present crisis; but even to a girl of her force of character, many of the details she had to carry out were painful and embarrassing in the extreme. On her shoulders fell the burden of settling with the servants, the land-steward, the very gamekeepers and watchers on the estate. She advertised the stock and farming implements; she sent the horses and carriages to Tattersalls'; she negotiated the rescue of her sister's pianoforte out of the general smash. It had been arranged that those young ladies should pay a visit to their aunt, and Helen packed up their things, and started them, nothing loath, by the railway, and furnished them with money for their journey. Her purse was nearly empty when she returned from the station, and, sitting down to rest after her labours, in the dreary waste of a dismantled home, she realised, for the first time, the loneliness and misery of her position.

She had borne up bravely while there was necessity for action, while her assumed cheerfulness and composure implied a tacit protest against the abuse poured on her father; but in the solitude of the big drawing-room, with the carpets up, and the furniture "put away," she fairly broke down, leaning her head against the chimney-piece, and crying like a child.

She never saw the Midcombe fly toiling up the avenue; she never heard it grinding round to the door; she was thinking rather bitterly that her young life's happiness had been sacrificed through no fault of hers; that she had been misunderstood, ill-treated; that even her father, whom she loved so dearly, had placed her in a position of humiliation and distress; that everybody was against her, and she had not a friend in the world, when a light step, the rustle of a dress, and a well-known voice, caused her to start and look up. The next moment, with a little faint cry, that showed how stout-hearted Helen had been tried, she was in the embrace of Mrs. Lascelles, with her head on that lady's shoulder, who did not refrain from shedding a few tears for company.

"My dear, you mustn't stay here another instant," exclaimed the latter. "Where are your things? Where is your maid? I've kept the fly, and you're to come back with me by the five o'clock train. Your father says so. I've got his letter here. No. Where have I put it? Don't explain, dear; I know everything. He told me all about it from the first, and I should have been down sooner but for those abominable excursion trains. Ring the bell. Send for all the servants there are left, and tell them to get your boxes ready immediately! You're to pay me a nice long visit, my precious! And oh! Helen, I've got so much to tell you!"

The girl was already smiling through her tears. Even in the midst of ruin it seemed no small consolation to have such a friend as this; and there was a hearty brightness about Mrs. Lascelles, not to be damped by the despondency of the most hopeless companion.

"How good of you to come!" she said. "How like you, and how unlike anybody else! I've had a deal of trouble here, but it's all over at last. I've managed everything for him the best way I could, and now I must go to poor papa, and take care of him in that miserable little French town."

"Poor papa, indeed!" echoed the other. "I've no patience with him! But, however, it's no use talking about that to *you*. Only, my dear, don't distress yourself unnecessarily about poor papa. He'll do very well, and there's no occasion for you to go abroad at all. We shall have him back in a week. Friends have turned up in the most unaccountable manner. How shall I ever tell you all about it? In the first place, Helen dear, I'm going to be married!"

"*You!*" exclaimed Helen, in accents of undisguised astonishment; adding, after a moment's pause, as good manners required, "I'm sure I wish you joy!"

"Thank ye, dear," was the off-hand answer; "and who d'ye think is the adversary, the what-d'ye-call-it—the happy man?"

Two little separate spasms of jealousy shot through Helen simultaneously. It couldn't be Frank Vanguard, surely! And if it could, what did that matter to her? Perhaps it was Sir Henry. Helen had long learned to consider papa as her own property, and I am not sure but that this pang was sharper than the other.

"Anybody I know?" she asked, trembling in her secret heart for the reply.

"You know him quite well," answered Mrs. Lascelles, laughing. "Indeed he's a great admirer of yours, and at one time—no, I won't tell stories, I never was jealous of you and Mr. Goldthred, although you're much younger and prettier than me."

Helen certainly gave a sigh of relief, while Mrs. Lascelles glanced, not without satisfaction, at her own radiant face and figure in the glass.

"I'm sure I don't know how it all came about," she said, still laughing. "But, however, there it is! It's a great fact, and upon my word I'm very glad of it. Now you know he's got plenty of money, Helen (though I didn't marry him for that, I've enough of my own), and, like the good fellow he is, he has promised to help your father through his difficulties. There's no sort of reason why you shouldn't all live here as formerly, but in the meantime it won't hurt those girls to go to their aunt for a bit (I hope she will keep them in order), and you are to come to No. 40 with me."

This was, indeed, good news. Helen could hardly believe her ears, and the young lady who now tripped lightly about the house, getting her things together, and busying herself to afford her visitor the indispensable cup of tea, was extremely unlike the forlorn damsel who had been paying off servants and poring over accounts the whole of that dreary, disheartening day.

But more comfort was yet in store for Helen, as if Fate, having punished her enough, had now relented in her favour. The tea was drunk, the fly was packed, and the ladies were driven to Midcombe Station, in the interchange of no more interesting communications than were compatible with the bustle of departure and the jingling of their vehicle ; but no sooner were they established in a first-class carriage, with the door locked, than Mrs. Lascelles, turning to her companion, asked, as though she were carrying on the thread of some previous conversation—

"And who do you think, Helen—who *do* you think I found in the station meaning to come down to you at Blackgrove? He was actually taking his ticket. But I wouldn't hear of it, of course, and ordered him at once to do nothing of the kind."

"Mr. Goldthred, I suppose," guessed Helen.

"Not a bad shot!" answered the other. "Yes, he wanted to come, too; and begged and prayed very hard yesterday. Of course I forbid him. I'm not particular, but still, my dear, *les convenances!* No, Goldthred knew he mustn't last night. It was Frank Vanguard I found fussing about on the platform this morning."

Hurt, wounded as she had been, in spite of all her pride, all her injuries, the tears rose in Helen's eyes, while she thought of her false lover hurrying down to take his share of her distress. Perhaps he was *not* false after all. Perhaps time would exonerate him, demonstrating, in some romantic and mysterious manner, that the unaccountable neglect she had so resented was not really his fault. She had been making excuses for him to her own heart ever since they parted. She was longing to forgive him fully and freely now.

But, unlike her companion, Miss Hallaton kept her feelings a long way below the surface, so it was a very calm, proud face she turned to Mrs. Lascelles, while in a perfectly unmoved tone she observed—

"Captain Vanguard is a great friend of papa's, and I am sure he would be very sorry to hear of our misfortunes."

"He *looked* it!" answered the other meaningly. "Poor fellow, he was as white as a sheet, and his face seemed almost haggard for so young a man! It can't be entirely smoking and late hours, for that plague of mine smokes and sits up like other people, yet he's got plenty of colour, and his eyes are as clear as yours or mine. I must say I like a man to look *fresh*. There's something wrong about Frank. He's sadly altered of late, and I can't quite make him out."

Miss Hallaton was looking steadfastly through the window, while she replied—

"I haven't remarked it. To be sure I've not seen him lately. He used to have very good spirits as far as I recollect."

"He's not been the same man since Jin disappeared," said Mrs. Lascelles, with malice prepense, no doubt, but possibly "cruel only to be kind." "Yet I'm by no means clear he had anything to do with that most mysterious business. He never could have shammed ignorance so naturally when we all consulted together, though I must say he seemed the least anxious of the party. I used sometimes to fancy he liked her, and sometimes I fancied it was somebody else. I think so still. What do *you* say, Helen?"

But Helen changed the subject, skilfully diverting her companion's thoughts to her approaching marriage, a topic of so engrossing a nature, that it lasted all the way to London, and was not half exhausted when interrupted by the *fiancée's* characteristic exclamation, as their train glided smoothly alongside the platform—

"What a goose he is! I knew he'd come to meet us! How pleased he'll be to see I've brought you. Helen, he's a dear fellow. He's as good as gold!"

He was as good as gold. Subject to the touchstone of happiness, Goldthred's character came out like a picture lit by gas. The tints were brighter, the lines more firmly marked, there appeared more depth, more meaning, more force and character in his whole composition, and Mrs. Lascelles, who had begun by pitying as much as she loved him, found the pity changed to respect, and the love grown stronger than ever. She was proud of him now, while he, exulting in the distinction, strove all the more to continue worthy of her good opinion.

Surely on earth there is no incentive to virtue so powerful as the entire affection of that one being who represents our ideal of some purer and higher sphere. The idol is mere clay, no doubt, but the divine spark exists at least in the worshipper; and it may be that the stubborn human heart, now in a dream of joy, now in an agony of suffering, is thus trained and taught to look up from the limited and imperfect creature, to the boundless attributes of the Creator.

After her late excitement and distress, Helen had much need of rest, both for body and mind. At No. 40 she found herself in a secure and peaceful haven, where even during the flood-tide of a London season, she might have

> "Listened to the roar
> Of the breakers on the bar outside that never reach the shore,"

but where in the hot dull autumn, when everybody was out of town, she could remain perfectly tranquil and undisturbed, with Mrs. Lascelles to humour her like a child, and Goldthred always ready to anticipate her lightest wish.

It did not take many days, before the firmness had returned to her step, the light to her eyes, and she was once more the "belle Helen," as Mrs. Lascelles loved to call her, with a vague notion the title was extremely classical and correct.

But it was quite contrary to the principles of the elder lady that any one who possessed health and beauty should be "mewed up," as she was pleased to express herself, while the weather tempted everybody out of doors. Sitting at luncheon, with Miss Hallaton on one side, and the faithful Goldthred on the other, she exclaimed, with the glee of an idle child who has found a new plaything, looking very bright and handsome the while—

"Happy thought! Let us drive down to-morrow to Oatlands! Weep at the dogs' graves, peep at the grotto, sit by the river, dine, and come back by moonlight. Who says *done?* It's almost the next thing to a water-party."

"Done!" exclaimed both her companions at the same moment, one with careless acquiescence, the other with intense admiration.

"Carried!" said the hostess, clapping her hands. "We three in the open carriage—*must* have a fourth. Who is it to be?"

But *one* was out of town, another couldn't get away early enough in the afternoon; *this* person wouldn't come without the certainty of meeting *that.* Of two charming sisters both must be asked or neither. In short, the fourth seat in the carriage was wanted for half-a-dozen people, and the prospective little dinner out of town soon assumed the dimensions of a pic-nic.

Thus it fell out that Mrs. Lascelles had to write several notes after luncheon, and "dear Helen" sat down to help her, while Goldthred, lounging about and failing sadly in his efforts to make the bullfinch pipe, volunteered to post these missives on his way to the club when they were finished.

Pocketing them all in a lump, and expressing his intention of returning at tea-time, Mr. Goldthred took his departure to walk down the street, with the jaunty step and lightsome air of a happy lover.

At the nearest pillar-post, he stopped to fulfil his promise, and being (though in love) a man of business, looked carefully at their addresses before dropping the letters one by one into the slide.

The very top-most was Helen's production,

and he started violently, the moment its superscription caught his eye. Hastily examining two more in the same handwriting, he replaced the whole in his pocket, hailed a Hansom and drove straight home, where he ran to his writing-table, unlocked a drawer and pulled out a certain little note that he had received one night at his club awhile ago, that had puzzled him exceedingly at the time, and that was, perhaps, the only secret he kept from Mrs. Lascelles, because he had found himself unable to explain it till to-day.

Yes, there could be no doubt, it was the same handwriting, he felt convinced, fully as ever was Malvolio. The unknown correspondent who wrote—"If you are really in earnest, come to-morrow; there is somebody to be consulted besides me," was Miss Hallaton! "There's something very queer about this," pondered Goldthred. "The girl's met with some foul play somewhere or another. It's all right now. I'll have it out with her to-night before I sleep—then I can tell my beautiful queen, and she will decide what ought to be done."

And Mr. Goldthred in his pre-occupation, forgetting to post the letters he had examined so carefully, brought them all back to No. 40 in his pocket, so that the expedition to Oatlands fell through after all.

CHAPTER XXX.

"REMORSEFUL."

MRS. LASCELLES was a lady who could ill-keep a secret. Such disclosures as those made in the boudoir after tea, when Helen had gone up-stairs to rest, roused alike her indignation and her sympathy; she would have cried for justice from the house-tops, rather than suffer the fraud to pass unexposed. Even Goldthred did not escape rebuke for the very negative part he had taken in the transaction.

"Why didn't you bring it here that instant?" she asked, in her pretty, imperious way, while she filled her admirer's tea-cup, and offered him the easiest chair in the room. "You shouldn't have kept such a thing from *me* for half-a-second. It's not like you to be so wicked, and I'm determined to scold you well!"

"But it was one o'clock in the morning," urged Goldthred, with a comical look of deprecation. "And you must remember I thought you didn't care a bit for me then. Of course it would be different *now*."

"That's nonsense," she exclaimed. "You know I always liked you; and as for your cool suggestion of coming here at one in the morning *now*, I beg you won't attempt anything of the kind. But you *ought* to have told me indeed, because, after all, the note might have been from somebody who had fallen in love with you!"

"I didn't suppose such a thing possible," he answered simply, "and I'm sure I didn't wish it. I used to think happiness was never intended for me. The one I liked seemed so much too good. I'm often afraid I shall wake and find it all a dream."

"Not half good enough," she murmured, making a great clatter among the cups and saucers. "I wish I was ten times better, and

I mean to be. But never mind about that. Don't you see exactly what has happened?"

"No, I don't," he answered, wondering fondly whether in Europe could be found such a pair of hands and arms as were hovering about the tea-tray under his nose. "I dare say I'm very stupid, but hang me if I can see daylight any-where!"

"Not if you look for it in my bracelet," she said, laughing. "But it's obvious Helen has written you a note intended for somebody else. Unless"—here she threatened him with a pretty finger he longed to kiss—"unless you have reason to believe she valued the admiration you could not disguise in all your looks and actions."

"Don't say such things!" he exclaimed, in the utmost alarm. "Mrs. Lascelles, do you think I'm—I'm *that* sort of fellow? Surely *you* know me better. Surely you are only in joke!"

"You're deep, sir," she continued, still laugh-ing at an earnestness that touched while it amused her. "Deep and sly! However, I'll believe you this time, and if you're honestly stupid I'll condescend to explain. Can you take in, that if the note wasn't written to *you* it must have been intended for somebody else? I can guess who that somebody is. I'll ask Helen point-blank. She's as proud as Lucifer, but I think she has confidence in me."

She *did* ask Helen point-blank, and that young lady, though as proud as Lucifer, condescended to own the truth, but accompanied her confession with a solemn declaration that everything was at an end between herself and Frank Vanguard, so that the great desire of her heart now was never to set eyes on him again. Mrs. Lascelles interpreting these sentiments in her own way, sat down forthwith, and penned the following little note, for further mystification of this bewildered young officer.

"DEAR CAPTAIN VANGUARD,—

"I have discovered something you ought to know. Such an *embrouillement* was never heard of but in an improbable farce, or still more improbable novel. Come to luncheon to-morrow, and we will lay our heads together in hopes of unravelling the skein. Miss Hallaton is staying with me. You will like to meet her I am sure, only you and I must have our conference *first*.

"Yours very sincerely,

"ROSE LASCELLES."

Frank's heart leaped under his cuirass while he read this mysterious epistle, on his return from a sweltering inspection in the Long Walk. He had been trying to persuade himself he did not care for Helen, and fancied he succeeded. It was humiliating to feel that the bare mention of her name could thus affect him, yet was there a keen, strange pleasure in the sensation nevertheless.

On the barrack-room table of this fortunate dragoon there lay however another little missive, bearing to that of Mrs. Lascelles the sort of likeness a pen-wiper has to a butterfly. Its envelope was squarer and larger, its monogram gaudier and more intricate, its superscription fainter, paler, more aslant, more illegible. It exhaled a strong odour of musk, and was written on paper that glistened like satin.

"Dear Frank," it ran, "I shall be in the park to-morrow, at twelve. Look for the pony-carriage. I *want* you—so no nonsense. Don't fail—there's a good fellow.—Yours truly,—KATE CREMORNE. P.S. If I'm not under the clock, wait there till I come."

"What can *she* be up to now?" thought Frank, carefully twisting this communication into a spill with which to light his cigar. "Got into a mess of some sort, no doubt, and expects me to pull her through, like the rest of them. How odd it is, I'm always blundering into entanglements with women I don't care two straws about, and the one I really *could* love, the one who would make me a good man, I do believe, and certainly a happy one, seems to be drifting every day farther and farther out of my reach. I shall see her to-morrow, and what then? I suppose our greeting will be confined to a distant bow, and some conventional sentence more painful than a cut direct. Still, I shall see her. That will be something. How strange it seems to be so easily satisfied now, when I think of all I hoped and expected so short a time ago. Well, beggars mustn't be choosers. I suppose I may as well meet Kate Cremorne first, and do her a turn if I can. She's a good girl, Kate, after all. Not half a bad-looking one neither, and as honest as the day."

So twelve o'clock found Frank very nicely dressed, and with a wonderfully prosperous air, considering his many troubles, picking his way daintily across the deserted Ride, to where a solitary pony-carriage, with a solitary pony drawing, and a solitary lady driving it, stood like a pretty toy, drawn up by the footway under the clock.

Miss Cremorne received him with coldness, even displeasure. She entertained a high opinion of her own acuteness, and thought she had hit upon a discovery by no means to his credit. In her many visits to Miss Ross—visits never made empty-handed, and to which, in all probability, the latter owed her restoration to health —she gathered from Jin that a friendship had lately existed between herself and the Captain Vanguard of whom they both loved to talk. Now, Belgravia and Brompton look at most matters in life, and particularly those connected with the affections, from different points of view. Kate, though a hybrid belonging to both districts, partook largely of the sentiments and feelings affected by the latter. She imagined a touching little romance, of which Jin's dark, curly-headed boy was the sequel, and being herself *sans peur*, determined to show Frank she did not hold him *sans reproche*.

"Jump in," said she, with extreme abruptness, as he approached the carriage. "I've got a crow to pick with you, and I mean to have it out. You're a nice young man, now! Don't you think you are?"

"Certainly," answered Frank, with imperturbable *bonhomie*. "I used to hope you thought so too!"

"I'll tell you what I used to think," said Kate, lashing the pony with considerable vehemence. "I used to think you were a good fellow at heart, though the nonsense had never been taken out of you; that you were only vain and affected on the surface, like lots of you guardsmen, but that there was a *man* inside the dandy, if one could only get at him. Oh, Captain Vanguard, I'm disappointed in you! If I cared two straws for a fellow, and he did as you've done, I'd never speak to him again! There!"

The whip was again dropped on the pony, and they shaved the wheels of an omnibus to an inch.

"Don't take it so to heart, Kate!" laughed Frank. "If I *have* deserted you, I'll come back again. You know, Miss Cremorne, that you are the only woman I ever loved, and all that. Fate has been obdurate; but rather would I be torn with wild——"

"*Will* you be serious?" demanded the fair charioteer, knitting her brows, and looking intensely austere. "Do you know where I am driving you now?"

He was incorrigible.

"To Gretna, I trust, or the Register Office. That's what I should like with *you*. Let's have it out, Kate. Jump over a broomstick, and the thing's done!"

"I'll tell you where you're going," she said gravely: "I am taking you to see Miss Ross!"

His whole countenance changed; and with all his self-command, he could not disguise how deeply he was agitated.

"Miss Ross!" he stammered. "You have heard from her! You know where she is!"

"I have *seen* her every day for the last fortnight," was the answer. "Seen her battle and bear up against sorrow, sickness, privation—actual want! Ay, many a day, when you've been sitting down to a dinner of four courses and dessert, that woman and her boy—her boy, Captain Vanguard—have not had enough to eat!"

"Great heavens, Kate!" he exclaimed. "This is too shocking! Why did I not know of it before?"

"Why, indeed!" repeated Kate. "You may

well ask yourself the question. Whose duty was it but yours to be answerable for her, poor dear, to find her a home, to provide for her and the child? I don't want to have many words about it. I'm not one of that sort; but I tell you she would have starved—yes—*starved*, if I hadn't happened to run against her by good luck, just in the nick of time."

"God bless you, Kate!"

His eyes were full of tears, and she looked at him a little less hardly than before, but answered in somewhat scornful accents—

"Ought such a job as that to have been left to *me?*"

"Miss Cremorne! Kate!" he urged; "you think worse of me than I deserve! There is nothing I wouldn't have done, no sacrifice I wouldn't have made, to ensure Miss Ross's comfort! It is not my fault, indeed! I give you my word of honour, I have left no stone unturned to discover her place of refuge from the moment she disappeared, and never obtained the slightest trace of her till to-day."

"Gammon!" replied Kate, pulling the pony short up by the kerbstone. "There's the house. It's not much to look at, but it's better inside than out, since she's found a chance friend, poor thing! Run up-stairs and see her. Say I meant to have taken her out for a drive, but I'll come again in the afternoon. I never did—I never will—believe you're a bad-hearted fellow, Frank; but you've done no end of mischief here. Go and undo it now."

So Kate drove off at high pressure, leaving Frank on the doorstep, confronting a maid-of-all-work, who, seeming to expect him, yet glanced from time to time with considerable interest and approval at his general appearance and outline.

He was shown into a clean, neatly furnished apartment, from which he could distinctly hear his announcement as "The gentleman, if you please, ma'am," and the rustle of a dress that followed this information. Then the door opened, and Miss Ross stopped short on the threshold, exclaiming only—

"Frank!"

The tone denoted nothing but extreme and overwhelming astonishment.

Looking in her face, he could not but admit she was sadly altered. A few short weeks had changed the brilliant, piquante beauty to a faded invalid, with wan, wasted features, lit up only by the wonderful black eyes.

His first thought was the humiliating question —"Can this be the woman I fancied I loved so dearly?" His second brought a manly and natural resolution to stand by her all the more firmly for her distress.

"Jin," he exclaimed, "why did you leave me like that? What has been the matter? and why didn't you trust entirely to *me?*"

He would have taken her in his arms, but she waved him off, and the delight that had flashed across her face when she confronted him gave way to a cold, unnatural reserve.

"Did you get my letter?" she asked. "And why are you here?"

He explained how and why he had come, touching on the disappointment he experienced in the contents of her communication, trying to put into his tones that warmth of affection which he felt was completely extinguished in his heart.

"I did not mean to see you again, Captain Vanguard," she said, in a measured voice; "I did not *wish* to see you again. The person I expected was your friend, Mr. Picard. That man stands between us, and always must. I will have no more concealments now—no more foul play—no more crime. I have been punished enough; I pray heaven I may not be punished yet more! I deceived you, Captain Vanguard, because I—well—I believe I *did* care for you, as much as it is in my wicked, heartless nature to care for anybody; but I meant you to marry me. And all the time Picard was my husband!"

"Your husband!" He had no power to utter another word.

"It takes your breath away," she exclaimed, with a touch of her old malice. "You are so innocent! so inexperienced! Frank, I believe you *did* mean honestly by me. I believe you thought you liked me; and I certainly—well—

I liked *you*. Horribly—shamefully! To win you, I was guilty of a fraud, a degradation, *une bassesse, entendez vous? une lâcheté*. I took the letter of a girl who loved you, and I sent it off to another man—a good creature, *mais tant soit peu ganache*, who didn't know what to make of it. Never mind. I detached you from her, and caught you for myself. But I would not make you a slave to my husband; I know him too well. None of us come out of this *imbroglio* very creditably, and, believe me, your part is not of the highest calibre; but I have injured you, and now, because my spirit is broke, I try to make reparation. Go to your Miss Hallaton; explain all to her; marry her, if you will! Oh! Frank, be happy with her, I entreat of you; and never come to see me any more!"

She looked in his face for about half a second, made a plunge at his hand, caught it eagerly to her heart, her eyes, her lips, and was in the next room, of which he heard the door locked and bolted, before he had realised the fact that she was gone.

He waited, he called, he went and tapped at that securely fortified retreat, he even rang for the servant, and begged her to ask the lady whether there were no more commands for him before he left; but without avail.

"Why the devil Kate brought me here," said Frank to himself, standing once more in the street, looking helplessly about for a Hansom cab, "is more than I can make out! One thing's clear—I'm not bound in any way to Miss Ross. Hang it! she's *not* Miss Ross! What a fool I've been! I don't deserve to get out of the mess so well. Helen, my darling! I ought to have known, if they hadn't got *at* you, you'd have been as true as steel! By Jove, though, I'm bound in honour to book up to Kate! It must have cost her a goodish stake, and I don't suppose Picard will."

But when this proposal was submitted to Miss Cremorne, she repudiated it with a contempt savouring of Belgravia, and an energy of expression not unworthy of Brompton.

CHAPTER XXXI.

REPENTANT.

Miss Ross, as we may still continue to call her, had indeed expected a visit from a gentleman, and warned the maid-of-all-work she would be at home; but it was with a heavy heart, nevertheless, she heard the street-door close on Frank's retreating steps, while, smoothing her hair and drying her eyes, she prepared to meet her husband. Picard, at his wits' end for money, hunted from place to place by writ and summons, with debts unpaid and bills coming due, could yet find time to answer in person a written request for an interview, made by the woman whose evil genius he seemed to have been through life. She asked to see him once more, for reasons to be explained in person, and was actually waiting his arrival, when Kate drove to the door with Frank Vanguard. The latter had hardly been gone five minutes, ere Picard made his appearance, and this ill-assorted couple met once more, with less surprise indeed, but scarcely more cordiality than they had shown during their strange ill-omened companionship on the river at Windsor.

Each thought the other looking faded, worn, altered; each wondered where had lain the attraction, once so fatally powerful; each, I think, was resolved at heart this interview should be the last.

"How's the boy?" said Picard, glancing round the room in search of his child.

For answer, she opened a door into the adjoining apartment, signing to him, wearily and sadly, to go in.

On a neat, snowy little bed, drawn near the open window, lay the child, wan, wasted, scarcely conscious; his large eyes wandering vaguely here and there, his small, fragile hands limp and helpless on the counterpane. He gave his mother a feeble glance of recognition; but of the other visitor he took no notice whatever.

Picard's mouth was dry, and a knot seemed to rise in his throat.

"How's this?" he muttered, in a fierce, husky voice, trying to keep down his tears by making himself angry. "The child is fearfully ill! It is too bad! I ought never to have trusted you with him! I should have thought his mother would have taken better care!"

The taunt was unfelt, unheeded. She showed no displeasure; but turned her large eyes on him with a plaintive, solemn sadness that spoke volumes, that told of dreary, waking nights, of anxious, sorrowing days, of cruel alternations between hope and despair, of piteous, calm resignation, that comes only when the last chance has faded gradually away. Picard went to the window, and looked out. A harder-hearted man probably did not walk the streets of London that day; but the one thing on earth he cared for was his child, and he saw the humble, dirty little street through a mist of tears.

"It is the only link between us *now*," said Jin, in a measured, mournful voice. "If it should part, God help us both! I do believe you care for that poor, pale, suffering darling. For *his* sake, let us forgive one another!"

He was touched, penitent, and for the moment a better man.

"Virginie," he said, "I have deceived you—doubly deceived you! Our marriage was valid enough."

Her heart sank within her.

"Then I am really your wife?" she faltered; but glancing at the boy, added bravely, "I will try to be a good one from this day forth."

A man's whole nature is not to be changed by a few tears and a minute's emotion. Dashing his hand across his eyes, Picard reviewed the position, and was his own bad self again. Less than ever would it suit him now to be hampered with the incumbrance of a family. He could scarce keep his head above water. To provide for mother and child would swamp him completely. While doing ample justice to his wife's sense of duty, he resolved by no means to imitate her; and with an assumption of great frankness, thus delivered himself—

"Your resolution is most creditable, Virginie, and I know to-day that I have never done you justice. But I have met lately with reverses, misfortunes, and at present it is impossible to make any arrangement by which you and I can be together as much as I might wish."

An expression of intense relief came over her weary face, yet she drew near the child's bed, suspiciously, instinctively, like an animal protecting its young.

He observed and understood the action.

"Our poor boy cannot be moved," said he. "You will be a good mother, Virginie, if I leave him to you? Perhaps I may never see him again."

Once more he betrayed real emotion; while Jin, from an impulse she could neither resist nor explain, raised the feeble little form on its bed, and supported the wan brow to which

Picard's lips clung in a long farewell kiss. He would have blessed the child had he dared; but with the half-formed prayer came a sense of shameful unworthiness and a bitter hopeless remorse that he had been so bad a man.

In true womanly unselfishness, and with a certain readiness of immediate resource peculiar to her sex, Jin made a mental calculation of her humble little store, reserving the small sum she thought would suffice till her boy's recovery, and offered the remainder ungrudgingly to her husband.

No doubt his excuses to himself were valid and unanswerable. He accepted it without hesitation, accepted, though he must have known it had been given her by another, and was all she had in the world.

To Jin, it seemed as if she had thus bought back the unquestioned possession of her child.

He wished her good-bye calmly and kindly enough, resolving, no doubt, that they should never meet on earth again; but, bad as he was, he cut a lock off that cluster of black curls tumbled on the pillow, and many a day afterwards would he take it out of his pocket-book to look on it for minutes at a time, with sad, repentant longing, that yet produced no good result. Sentiment is not affection. There may be much romance, with very little attachment; and many a man believes he is extremely fond of a woman or a child, for whom he will not sacrifice a momentary gratification or an hour's amusement.

When Picard went his way, Jin clasped the boy in her arms, as if he had just been rescued from some imminent danger; nor could all Kate Cremorne's persuasions, calling an hour afterwards in the pony-carriage, induce her to leave him during the rest of the afternoon.

It was for no want of nursing, from no lack of care and culture, that this poor little flower faded and withered away.

August waned into September, and still the child drooped with the drooping leaves. To the doctor, to the landlady, to the weeping maid-of-all-work, to every one, save only a mother, it was evident that his Christmas carols would be sung to him by the angels in heaven.

But though here a poor little violet may be trampled into earth, is that a reason why the fairest garden flowers should fail to bloom, fragrant and splendid, over yonder? Never a red rose in all the garlands of the house of Lancaster blushed so becomingly, to Goldthred's taste, as did his own affianced bride when she ordered him to ask her whether she had not better think about naming the day of their marriage.

It was fixed for the middle of the month, the lady arranging to spend her honeymoon at a farm-house of her own, far off in the West of England, where there was excellent partridge-shooting. She explained her arrangements to Helen with characteristic frankness.

"You see, my dear, I've been married before, and I know what it is. When Mr. Lascelles and I were alone together, the first week, it was *awful!* I wouldn't have believed man or woman could be so bored, and live. He must have hated it, and, I'm sure, so did I. Now, I don't want my goldfinch to be bored with *me*, particularly at first; so I shall send him out shooting. He'll come home tired and hungry, and we shall make no fuss, but feel as if we'd been married for years. 'Pon my word, dear, he's such a good fellow, I wish we had!"

To all which wisdom, gathered from experience, Helen turned an attentive ear, because of the pleadings urged by a certain young officer, who felt and owned himself unworthy of the happiness he implored day by day, hour by hour, till she contradicted him flatly, out of the fulness of her own heart. Frank Vanguard succeeded in justifying himself before an exceedingly lenient tribunal; and although, in my opinion, the unaccountable silence of one woman is no valid excuse for transferring allegiance incontinently to another, I do not imagine ladies themselves are equally exclusive in their notions of property. They affect a very stringent law of trespass, no doubt; yet appear sufficiently merciful to habitual and hardened offenders.

The most jealous of them seem to appreciate an admirer none the less that he has offered incense at many foreign shrines. If he should have tumbled a goddess or two off her pedestal, they profess themselves shocked indeed, and are loud in reproof, but seem to like him all the better for his infidelity.

So Frank and Helen were to be married, Sir Henry giving them his blessing and the bride's *trousseaux*, for which tasteful and magnificent outfit the bills were eventually sent in to Frank; but this has nothing to do with our story. The cavalry officer, I venture to pronounce, had better luck than he deserved; but so exemplary a daughter as Helen had proved herself was pretty sure to make an exemplary wife. And, for my own part, I believe that a good woman, with good sense, and a *really* good temper, especially if gifted also with good looks, is capable of reclaiming the whole Household Brigade, horse and foot, bands, trumpeters, drummers, officers, non-commissioned officers, and men.

Sir Henry Hallaton, however, with gross injustice, laid his ruin on that sex, to which he had devoted what he was pleased to call the *best* years of his life, majestically ignoring all such deteriorating influences as extravagant habits, dissipated company, gambling, mortgages, second-rate race-horses, and protested bills.

It needed no syren to lure the baronet on the rocks; and, indeed, the tide of fortune, whether it ebbed or flowed, seemed alike to waft this reckless, easy-going mariner to certain ship-wreck. His was a sadly shattered bark now, and he had abandoned all idea of making safe anchorage at last. He came back to England, rescued from ruin by the timely aid of a friend, and thought himself ill-used because that friend was on the eve of marriage with a woman whom he had neglected while he thought she liked him, to whose heartlessness, he now told himself, he was a martyr, because she had not waited for an uncertainty, but made a wise choice in pleasing herself.

The daughter he loved so dearly was about to settle happily in life; ye he could complain that he was deserted, bewailing his loneliness, though he saw the light in her eye, the peace on her brow, that told of heart's-ease and content. In the restless, dissatisfied longings of a confirmed selfishness, he tried hard to re-establish his former intimacy with Miss Ross, whose retreat he had found means to discover; and, failing to obtain an interview with that anxious and afflicted woman, found himself driven for solace and comfort to the society of Kate Cremorne.

This young person, whose knowledge of the world was drawn from men, not books, seeing through the weary, worn-out pleasure-seeker at a glance, fooled him with considerable dexterity, and no little mischievous amusement.

Of all his reckless moods, perhaps none had been so reckless as that in which he offered to make so free-spoken a damsel his wife; of all his humiliations none, perhaps, so galling as to accept a kindly, courteous, and dignified refusal from the wild, wayward girl, who bade him understand clearly that she respected herself too much to affect an attachment it was impossible to feel for a man old enough to be her father!

Mrs. Battersea was provoked, and opined Kate would never grow wiser, but Sir Henry, while to the outward world his good humour and good spirits remained unchanged, took the rebuff sorely to heart, and though he told his doctor he had been drinking sweet champagne, which never agreed with him, my own belief is that a fit of gout, which attacked him at this juncture more sharply than usual, was the effect of love rather than wine. When we begin twinges at the extremities, it is time to have done with pains of the heart.

So his doctor ordered him to Buxton, where, soothed by the bubble of those health-restoring springs, he forgot his sorrows in the unintermittent attention to self, required by the constant ablutions and daily discipline of the cure, deriving at the same time no small comfort from the contemplation of many sufferers more crippled, more peevish, more egotistical than himself.

There is no particular season at Buxton, as

there is no forgiveness or immunity from Podagra, goddess of sloth, and luxury, and excess. Its waters are drunk, its baths are heated, its lodging-houses occupied, its parade populous, during every month of the year. Nevertheless its frequenters are necessarily migratory. Those who get better go away, those who get worse die; but disease sends in a continuous supply of fresh afflictions, and the residence of a very few weeks causes a patient to be looked on as an old inhabitant and high authority in the place. The head of the *table-d'hôte*, the easiest chair on the parade, the newest books from the library, the choicest game from the poulterer, the sweetest smile from landlady, the lowest bow from landlord, are the advantages to be attained by six weeks' tenure of an obstinate case; and thus it came to pass that Sir Henry, though a far greater man in St. James's Street, found he could not hold a candle to Uncle Joseph at Buxton.

Like two veterans in Chelsea, like two old man-of-war's men in Greenwich Hospital, these campaigners of a less honourable warfare found themselves stranded in sadly shattered plight amongst the bare knolls and grey boulders of the Derbyshire Peak; but between them there was this important difference,—that whereas Sir Henry, still almost handsome, still gentlemanlike, amusing, pleasant to women, had loved his love, gamed his gaming, and retired beaten from the strife; Uncle Joseph, older in years, ruder in speech, rounder of form, and stouter of heart, had refitted his shattered bark, and with favouring gales, backed by an energy that cannot be too highly commended, was prosecuting his suit with a widow almost as old, as round, and as gouty as himself.

There had been a time when Sir Henry would have laughed heartily at the confidential communications made by the respectable Mr. Groves, as the two drove out in a one-horse fly and halted to enjoy the mellow warmth of an autumn sun under a chasm, which takes from its impossible legend the name of the Lover's Leap; but he did not laugh to-day, listening with attention, interest, something akin to envy, at his heart.

What would he not have given could he, too, take pleasure in a woman's smile, even though the woman were old and fat; could he, too, feel his blood course quicker at a woman's voice, even though it had a provincial accent, and an occasional confusion of the rules by which the aspirate is applied in our language?

"I congratulate you," said Sir Henry, lying languidly back in the carriage with a plaintive air of resignation, and a sad conviction that for him most pleasures were indeed over, since his doctor had even forbidden him to smoke. "You have retained the best faculties of youth, since you have still courage to hope, still energy to be vexed and disappointed. It is not so with me. Look here, my dear fellow; I have been ruined twice since I began, and twice set on my legs by a miracle. I would willingly be ruined a third time, and never be set up at all, if I could only take a real interest in any earthly thing, even in what I am going to have for dinner."

Uncle Joseph stared. "It's not so with me," he answered; "far from it. I wish I didn't care so much. I'm a desperate fidget sometimes, I know, and often I can't enjoy things just for fear of what *might* happen. Perhaps it's because I'm an old bachelor, as they say. It's a great drawback to a man in middle-age to have passed all his youth out of the society of women."

Sir Henry smiled and shook his head.

"I haven't found the *other* plan a good one," said he. "You and I have been a goodish time in the world now, and I begin to think we have both wasted our lives."

CHAPTER XXXII.

"RECLAIMED."

Day after day, week after week, an autumn sun glared fiercely down, baking and cracking the clean shorn stubbles, burnishing the meadows, all parched and smooth and shining, licking up with fiery thirst the shrunken threads of mountain streams, scorching the heather bloom to powder, burning to rich ripeness the strips of late-sown oats that through our wild hill-countries fringe the purple moorland with a border of gold, beating on heated wall and glowing pavement in the small close streets about the Marlborough Road, drying the outer air to the temperature of an oven, and withering without pity the humble little growth of migniouette in the sick child's window.

Morning and night Jin watered that homely box of mould in vain. The dying plants no more revived for her care, than did her darling for all the tears she shed on his behalf. They wanted for nothing now that money could supply,—Kate Cremorne would have taken care of that; but Jin's friends, directly they found out her hiding-place, had rallied round her with kindly offers of sympathy and assistance. Mrs. Lascelles, indeed, wished to bring mother and child home to No. 40 at once, but the latter was too ill to be moved; and kind-hearted Rose, in spite of her present happiness, felt sadly vexed to think that the former could refuse persistently to see her now, denying herself to every human being except Miss Cremorne.

With all her resolution it was more than Jin could endure to be reminded of the happiness she had once so nearly grasped, and in her dull, forlorn misery she told herself it was better to hide her weary head, and wait in hopeless apathy for the end.

She had gone through those cruel changes

that seem so hard to bear till the one fearful certainty teaches us they were merciful preparations for that which we should not otherwise have found strength to encounter. She had watched the doctor's face day by day, and hung on his grave, sympathising accents, believing now that the "shade better" meant recovery, now that the "trifle worse" was but the necessary ebb and flow of disease; anon, lifted to unreasonable happiness from darkest despair, because when her ignorance thought all was over, the man of science still found anchorage for a new ephemeral hope.

Alas! that henceforth there must be no more vicissitude, no more uncertainty! The last strand of the cable was obviously parting—the little lamp was flickering with the gleam that so surely goes out in utter darkness—the simple flower, drooping and dying, was to bloom never more but in the gardens of God!

Even Kate, who seldom failed to find a word of comfort at the worst, to discover seeds of encouragement in the most alarming symptoms, had turned from the boy's bed to-day with a quiver over all her bonny face, that showed how hard it was for her to keep back the tears.

Jin caught her friend's hand, and pressed it to her breast.

"God bless you, dear!" she gasped. "Whatever happens, you've been an angel from heaven to me!"

The other dropped her veil till it covered brow and face.

"My poor dear!" she answered, with a strange tremor in her voice, "the angels in heaven are like *him*, not *me*. If it *must* be—if you *are* to lose him—try and think of him as one of them—try and hope you and I may get to see him there at last, even if we have to sit waiting for ages on a stone outside the gate."

Both women were silent, Kate turning away to cry passionately. In a few minutes she recovered herself, pressed her lips fiercely to the child's cold hand lying helpless on the bedclothes, again to Jin's pale, sorrowing brow, and so departed, with a promise, in a husky, choking whisper, of returning speedily, and an entreaty that she might be sent for at a moment's notice if she were wanted.

So the mother was left alone with her dying child. She had not shed a tear—no—though the other woman wept without restraint; that infection, usually so irresistible, had failed to reach her now. Her eyes were dry, her face cold and fixed like marble. Mechanically she moved about the room, arranging the furniture, straightening the sheets, smoothing the pillows, mixing a cooling drink for the poor pale lips that would never drink again. Then, as in unconscious routine she watered the mignionette at the window, she caught her breath with a great gasp, her face worked like that of a woman in convulsions, and she burst into a fit of weeping that seemed intense relief for the moment, and rendered her capable of enduring the worst, which was yet to come.

In such paroxysms memory seems, as it were, to lift us out of the present, and furnishing us with a new sense—keen, subtle, and intense—

throws our whole existence back once more into the past. Again she was nursing Gustave under the poplars in Touraine; again she was impressing on a homely peasant-woman, at Lyons, the care and culture of her darling; again she mourned for his loss and rejoiced in his recovery, staring with incredulous pleasure to recognise him on the road to Ascot, thrilling with a mother's holiest instincts to fold him to her breast in the old cottage by the river-side. Her troubles, her intrigues, her love, her rivalry, Picard, Frank Vanguard, Helen herself, were forgotten; no human interest, no earthly image, came between her and her dark-eyed boy.

It seemed impossible he could be dying. Dying? Oh, no! or why had he been given back to her before? Was there no Providence? Was it only blind chance that thus juggled with her? She thought of women she had known in her earlier years—*femmes croyantes*, as they called themselves—their penances, duties, attendance at mass, frequent confessions, and the courage with which they boasted their religion enabled them to accept every trial—till it came.

Pain was lashing her into rebellion. She roused herself. She dashed the tears from her eyes. "Bah!" she exclaimed; "if he gets well, I will be like these. Why not for me also a miracle? What have I done that I am to be so tortured?"

A weak voice called her from the bed. "Maman," it murmured, in the dear French accents of its infancy, "embrasse-moi donc, puis ce que je ne te vois plus."

She laid her head—the two black comely heads together—on the pillow by his side. The hope that had flickered for a moment died out for evermore. Not see her! and it was broad noon of the golden summer day!

"Here is mamma, darling!" she murmured, pressing hard to her lips the little helpless hand, dull and yellow like waxwork. "Mamma will never leave Gustave! never—never!"

She tried to borrow courage from the assurance, and to fancy that *he* was not leaving *her*, swiftly, surely, as the outward-bound bark that spreads its canvas to a wind off shore.

He nestled nearer—nearer yet. His little frame shook all over. Raising him on the pillow, his curly head sank back on her bosom, more heavily, more helplessly than in earliest infancy. He murmured a few indistinct syllables. Straining every nerve to listen, she knew they formed part of a child's prayer that Mrs. Mole had taught him in her cottage home.

But he finished that prayer at the feet of his Father who is in heaven.

Minutes, hours—she never knew how long—the sorrowing mother bowed her head, and wailed in agony over her dead child. Neither stunned nor stupefied by an affliction for which her daily life had of late been but a training and a preparation, every nerve in her frame, every fibre of her heart, quivered with the sting and sharpness of the blow.

Had she not wept, she must have gone mad; but her tears flowed freely, and with tears came that lassitude of the feelings which is the first step to resignation, as lacking the rebellious energy of despair. For her, indeed, the silver cord was loosed, the golden bowl broken, the desire of her eyes taken away. The day had gone down; the night seemed very dark and cold. How should she seek for comfort in the hope of another dawn?

But when the skies are at their blackest, then morning is near at hand. It was through thickest gloom, brooding over a lowering wave, that the luminous figure of their Teacher walked the waters on the Sea of Tiberias, and the boldest of his servants had sunk to the knees ere he took refuge in his panic-stricken outcry, "Lord, save me!" and, trusting solely to the Master, found help in the very weakness of his fears.

Perhaps angels in heaven recognise and mark in golden letters the hour of conviction, the accepted time, the turning-point, it may be, of a soul's eternity. Perhaps, even, in their lustrous happiness, they rejoiced with celestial sympathy over the lonely penitent who flung herself down by her child's death-bed, and poured out her heart in prayer that, through any sacrifice, any suffering, she might follow where he was gone before. Perhaps they knew how poor, contrite, sorrowing Jin Ross had made her first step on the narrow path that leads to the Shining Gate, over which, for sinners of far deeper dye than her, stands emblazoned the eternal promise—"Knock, and it shall be opened unto you!"

THE END.

PRINTED BY VIRTUE AND CO., CITY ROAD, LONDON.

www.ingramcontent.com/pod-product-compliance
Lightning Source LLC
Chambersburg PA
CBHW030619030726
47497CB00006B/1563

9783337379858